THE
SANDWICHED

Abhitabh D. Honap

Clever Fox PUBLISHING
Chennai • Bangalore

CLEVER FOX PUBLISHING
Chennai, India

Published by CLEVER FOX PUBLISHING 2026

ISBN: 978-93-7500-610-7

PROLOGUE

Shalini and Santosh were in their fifties. Both highly educated, worked at senior positions in their careers.

Shalini married Santosh just under quarter of a century ago. Santosh fell for her ever since he saw her for the first time. Both were intelligent, responsible, belonged to the same caste and even their parents too had no reason to turn their marriage proposal down. Shalini had a younger sibling, whereas Santosh was the only child.

Shalini gave birth to Shaunak just after first few years of their marriage. They stayed in Bengaluru after their wedding and were almost local Kannadigas by then. Shaunak, now in his twenties, remained the only child of the couple, fondly raised and had won a demographic jackpot, being born to such intelligent, well-heeled parents.

Shaunak was not as intelligent as his parents and had been a below-average performer. Shalini wanted to make Shaunak her piece of aim, to be special. Santosh, on the other hand, appeared to have wanted to let Shaunak be his own. The family of three hung out on the weekends, had developed a fastidious and merry-making circle of friends, all almost of the same genre as theirs, and spent time in gay whenever they could.

Shaunak, a *Gen Zee* illustrator, was attached to problems that are sometimes abetted to his age; insecurity, lack of motivation, feeling of purposelessness or even despair. That made Shalini worried. She wanted Shaunak to be an ideal son, an excellent achiever, and a symbol of pride for a successful pair of parents.

Shalini herself, at that age, underwent swings of mood, got swayed by disturbances, in office and home too, which she could handle with aplomb, only just a decade back. She expected her to be managing much better force than she was doing today but had to digest mediocre performance ratings in the last few years. She was reaching a saturation point. Her superior was influenced by some of her other colleagues, which made her path further gruesome. All this, Shaunak, and her growing age, adorned by changing work scenario and dynamics, was making her start to lose belief in her capabilities and she unknowingly found herself trapped in the mirage of quagmire. Santosh had been her place to rely and relay.

Santosh appeared to be happy-go-lucky and had an enviable path of career, which matched Shalini's. Though he had had his ups and downs, he had clinched to his strengths and had found his way out, each time. He did not express, but he too was a little concerned and focused on Shaunak.

Shaunak had been brought up, all by his parents in the cosmopolitan and imposing city of Bengaluru. The Upadhayay family of Shalini, Santosh and Shaunak were an epitome of the changing nuclear family of modern times. Shaunak had occasional acquaintances with his grandparents, but only rarely, on special occasions. Santosh's parents were ailing and so were Shalini's. Shalini's younger sister Shweta, based in Delhi, had married Arjun and was now with their daughter, Siya. Both, the senior Upadhyayas and the senior Purohits were staying in Mumbai.

Shaunak

Shaunak woke up late, as every day. But he continued to roll over in the bed, crumpling the sheets so much as if to doubt if they were plain and ironed anytime back. He was half over the quilt and covered by the rest. His right bare calf had gotten quite cold due to the draught of the air conditioner straight hitting him. That was making him uncomfortable, but he persisted to cling to the bed, almost with a pre-decided, purposeful, obstinate intent to stay asleep. Shalini once again gave him a loud yell to disperse from the bed, and Shaunak, with a reluctant grunt, eventually gave in. He almost crawled to the bathroom, leaving behind a messy bed and equally messy side table, full of bands, wallet, coins, tissues, toothpicks, a small entangled world of charging cables and a box of mints.

After one more reminder from the kitchen, Shaunak moved his heels away from the commode, flushed the toilet without glancing a bit, and headed forward. He had a majestic bathroom. The shining golden fittings made his bathroom even dressier. His commode seat was his throne where he made grand strategies for the day and for the near term. After the first act of the day, Shaunak dragged himself to the mirror. He could see a few pimples on the right side of his right brow. His moustache was unkempt, beard uneven, and his sideburns were dark, long, deep, and thick. His hair had grown so much that his last trip to the hair stylist could have been several months back. Shaunak was fair, taller than Santosh, sturdily built, with a thick nose. His nostrils often stayed red, and eyes looked bright but tired.

Shaunak flossed, brushed his braced teeth judiciously, moistened his face with a spray of cool water, rubbed his eyes with care, and got ready to move out for another day, waiting for him to unfold.

The breakfast table waited anxiously for Shaunak, laden with cereals, milk, cut fruits, and some bread and spread. Yogini came early at Shalini's kitchen and cooked breakfast and lunch for their tiffins to be carried with. Shaunak sunk his neck into his mobile screen and started gulping spoonfuls of warm milk-drenched cereals, as fast as he could. Taste did not matter to him. And within no time, Shaunak had bottomed up his bowl of cereals, to give his empty stomach the tonic for the morning. Even as he swiped the last bit from the bowl, his penchant for his beloved screen did not fade.

He was a master at operating his mobile handset. His handset, the latest creation of one of the most famous brands, had a sizzling titanium gold frame, with a powerful memory, latest generation Snapdragon processor, and an excellent camera. It was one of the most sought-after devices in his contemporary generation. He cherished this new possession which landed into his lap on his twenty-first birthday, earlier in the month. After spending some crumbled moments on the mobile, he rose for his courtroom again, to bathe.

He was born two decades ago, in Mumbai, when Shalini returned to her parents' home in Goregaon to nurture her first pregnancy, just after settling down in Bengaluru. Santosh all but made up for the absence of Shalini by shuttling between Mumbai and Bengaluru, hopping between two homes when he was in Mumbai, one in Goregaon and the other in Khar, his parents' home.

When Shalini went into labour pains, Santosh was all by her side and watched the first of the next-gen of both the families evolve, all to the happiness and excitement of each of the Upadhayay and Purohit souls. Shaunak, as fair and cute as newborn babies are, was the darling of each member of the coterie. His even an innocuous act, drew up furls of pleasure and praise. Shalini's younger sister, who was in her early twenties then, was exceptionally fond of baby Shaunak and spent hours with him, doing all the mundane tasks too, with cheerful promptness.

Afterall, a baby was born in the house after two quiet decades.

Shweta was on the verge of finishing her graduation in dentistry and aiming for her master's very soon. She adored her nephew, all right. As coming of age, when she had some self-reflective, private moments, she secretly imagined her undergoing motherhood in some years to come and often blushed with that vicarious feeling.

Shaunak showered merrily, dressed up in summer cool whites, and royal-blue low-waist jeans, made his hair, only just, only to keep the comb in his room; happy, picked up his stuff from the disorderly side table, appended his sack to his right shoulder and headed towards the shoe rack. His beard remained uneven and unkempt to hand him over a pseudo-macho look, as if he wanted to carry it intentionally.

Shalini and Santosh both had preceded him to exit the home for work. They worked their way through the Bengaluru traffic to reach their offices, almost sapped, but vitalised themselves somehow, as they got into their office elevators, to stay over the day, surviving all the work challenges.

Shaunak had on his shoes and picked up his bike keys. It turned out to be the day for the blue sneakers. His bike, sullied but standing proud, was a monster powered by a 400cc BS6 engine, which developed a power of 45 bhp and a torque of around 40 Nm. The beast weighed around 170 kg. Fuel efficiency was not even an area of concern for any of the Bengaluru resident Upadhyayas, but the riding flamboyance was, more for Shaunak, indeed.

Shaunak had been studying at Lady Shreemoyi College and accumulating credits in the field of commerce and accounting. Shalini wanted him to carry his basket of credits to the US and ice his commerce-laden pastry with specialisation sourced from an US university. He had been tacitly living up to Shalini's dream and quite pervious to the fact that admission to such universities needed a good GPA score, to begin with, to get admitted handsomely.

Shaunak, like any other higher middle-class born kid, had fewer things to worry about, his cost of education, the least. He zoomed past his apartment complex gate and braked only at their rendezvous, where Tushar and Sayona greeted him with an animated wave. His fresh lime and lavender body odour did not spare the other tables seated by. Tushar was dressed in a polo T-shirt with tattered blue jeans. Sayona was smartly dressed in lavender, fresh colored polka dot top, and black trousers. With Shaunak joining that table, that table was readying to be one of the most colourful and happening tables at *the Fromer's*.

Sayona was infatuated with Shaunak, and she glanced at him blushingly as he swung his right leg over the bike to get off. As he took off his shades, she flushed from within without letting Tushar know. She would always grope to find out if Shaunak had similar feelings for her. Shaunak landed on the table of his peers in a scuff. He exclaimed, "I need to attend the boring accounting lecture, as Maddy is going to spread over the paper pattern today." In the multidisciplinary Shreemoyi College, Tushar was studying Indology and Sayona, Mass Communications.

Tushar was the son of the Mathurs, one of the family friends of Shalini and Santosh. Tushar's father, Rupesh, was Santosh's colleague when they both worked with an IT giant a few years back. They got along well and extended their office relationship beyond, into homes. They met often, over the weekends as families. Shaunak and Tushar, in a way, had grown up together. Tushar's mother, Preeti, was an architect and worked with a large architectural engineering firm. Preeti too got along with Shalini very well.

The young trio would meet daily at the *Fromer's* and start their day, often with a coffee or a shared sandwich. Today, they were relishing on a shared grilled sandwich, with cheesy mushrooms, dunked in garlic mayo, seasoned with basil and herbs, buttered delicately to send the aroma straight into the throat. As Shaunak picked up the last nugget of the sandwich, he stared at it, as if to check if any mayo kept hanging out, to soil his hands or drop off on the table. He continued to stare and imagined himself as a sandwich, stuffed with herbs, mushrooms and mayo hanging out.

He felt as if the sandwich portrayed him as one who was indeed sandwiched. As he continued to ride down the imagination, he became oblivious to the fact that Tushar and Sayona sat with him. He persisted with his thoughts and believed that he was grill-sandwiched, sandwiched between hope and despair, between herb and basil of expectations and bread slices of confusion, between cheesy mushroomed aspiration and lack of purpose. He felt helpless to be sandwiched between his inability to cope and the prospects he was looked upon with. He realised that this was making him frown, diffident and rebelliously purposeless.

Shaunak knew he had got whatever he wanted and would continue to get so as long as he wished and his parents could, so he never sketched the portrait on his aspirational canvas, too broad. He had confusedly reconciled to himself that he was not worthy of achieving anything bigger, and his lack of effort echoed his understanding. However, deep down within, he carried a remorse, a guilt of being a lower performer, but no sooner did he get something he had wished without much vying, than his remorse hibernated like a stomach-full bear.

Whenever he gathered himself again to prove himself, any such serious intent got killed in the bud stage itself.

Shaunak knew he was struggling from within, but could not comprehend what it really was, and whether there was. He was passing through an age zone where seriousness and responsibilities only resided with those compelled by circumstances. Actions out of choice remained a distant second, directly proportional to inner drive and conviction to perform. Shaunak struggled to imbibe the drive to perform. When alone and pensive, he wondered what would keep him going. He was weighing himself under the weight of expectations. Not that he did not want it himself, but every time he pressed himself forward, some creaky lack of effort kept him bound. So much so that his ability to put effort faded each time he took a step forward.

Shaunak gulped the last bite of the sandwich, which no longer looked as delectable and presentable as it was when it landed on the table; fresh and untouched. Vinayaka, the regular table keeper who by then knew them so well, just uttered three hundred and ten, and the three friends picked up that tab in equal shares, as they did every day. Shaunak paid those extra ten over 'The hundred per head share' and additionally paid twenty bucks to Vinayaka to make him give them special attention the day after and days to come. Vinayaka greeted the trio with a cheerful smile each time they visited *the Fromer's*, and that made them feel special and cared.

As he flunked his side stand and readied on his bike, Sayona jumped at the pillion seat, almost squeezing over him, to smell his lime and lavender afresh. Shaunak felt no excitement in that touch, as the bike roared with the kick, leaving a gust of smoke, powerfully exhausted in the air, to zoom past *the Fromer's*, to catch up with Maddy and his thrusted upon Accountancy II, and its silhouettes.

Shalini

It was destiny that brought Shailini from Mumbai to Bengaluru. It was well past ten on the Sunday night, and Shalini was engrossed in giving final touches to the presentation deck, which Murugan wanted her to send that evening itself, to be presented to their Vice President, the next day. Murugan had at least five rounds with her, virtually during the entire Sunday. Santosh could understand her ordeal as he too got into that tangle quite often with Rajeev Mohan.

Since morning, Shalini had made so many subtle changes to the deck, but was utterly unsuccessful in pleasing Murugan, any time over. Shalini's project was going south, and the profitability was sliding even further south. She and Murugan were vying for resources in an already despairing sheet, to bring it on track as it spiralled into a venomous jumble. More than twenty times on that sunny Sunday, Shalini felt like just quitting her job. The helplessness, despair, irritation, frustration, and anger were evident all through the day, in her demeanour and actions. Her attention to cooking a Sunday afternoon meal was the least, her interest to house-keep her wardrobe, which she initiated on Sundays, was shattered, not to sidestep her small altercations with Santosh and Shaunak even on petty matters.

Santosh tried his best to accommodate her circumstances, but even he caved in at some stage and that led to a vehement, aggressive skirmish around four in the evening. Both were acknowledging from within the real culprit, but the conceit and the battle of pseudo-upmanship, only for the sake of it, kept them going too far. Shalini, her laptop, the superfast 100 Mbps internet and Murugan's periodic commentaries, many of them unpleasant though, had a grand alliance on that day and it kept her Sunday till late evening, mundane and obligatory.

Shalini hit the "send" button on her Outlook almost at eleven, after she received the go-ahead from Murugan. She had her fingers aching, stiff, and her head began to feel quite heavy. She was in dire need of a shower. She switched on the boiler and waited for the water to heat up. Till then, she quickly made some hair, which was the evidence of her pitiful day thus far. At the green on the boiler, Shalini dashed into the bathroom. As she drenched herself under the warm water, raining from the shower overhead, she was crying from within. Her eyes closed, she wanted to shed some tears which would have flown secretly along with the bathing water. She was exhausted.

This was not the first time Shalini was slogging through such work. She had had several such endeavours in the past, but when she would hit the bed, she would sleep with a sense of achievement. However, today, she was totally sapped, more in her mind. She was growing older, walking on the tight rope of mid-age. She aspired to grow and fight around her ageing body and menopausal challenges, a growing son, who offered little confidence even as he rambled in his early twenties. All this package took a toll on her that Sunday, and Murugan became the designer and the architect of it that day.

She was soaking herself with just the right lukewarm water for quite some time and felt that it should have continued for eternity. At the first touch of the warm water over her neck and the back, she expressed a sigh, as if to yell out a rebel rumble. After some listless moments, Shalini came back to her senses, shut the shower tap off, wiped the excess water from her face and stretched to fetch the towel. She first wiped the condensed steam from the mirror to have a clear look at herself. As she started to wipe her face, she distinctly found the crow's feet around her eyes, with remarkable dark circles. That sight made her nervous. She rose to finish her bath chore and came out, with a warm, rose aroma, clad in the evening gown.

As she walked out, she desired a coffee served. Annoying Santosh earlier in the day, cut her that avenue. She wanted to drag herself to the kitchen, but could not decide. Eventually, she gave up the idea of coffee. She felt she had forgone too many of her desires by then, so why cling to a mere coffee? In the vulnerable and docile frame of mind, she started pitying herself for all the past matters in which she felt she was victimised. Murugan, in fact, was the silent catalyst to that situation.

She was moaning silently with that pain, and due to the strenuous efforts and topsy turvy journey of the mind the whole day, she went to sleep even without realising it. She did not even sense when Santosh came and slept beside her. She thought she had been sleeping for too long when the phone alarm rang mercilessly at the time, it was commanded to. She stretched her hand and snoozed it, out of habit. After a couple of snoozes, she gave in and swirled her sheet aside to rise for another stressful day, as she was anticipating.

The presentation went well, which meant Murugan and team got only the anticipated flak, not more. Nothing more than the worst they would have foreseen. So, Murugan, as seasoned a campaigner as he was, was content. He laid ease on Shalini and her peers. The Project they worked on was out of budget, low on client satisfaction, but lived to die another day. The management was forthright to extend some resource support, more as a humane gesture, than hope. They read out the writing on the wall, quite loudly to Murugan and his camp. That was not the first time Shalini was part of such a mess, but now it was taking more toll on her. As she shelved off the bashing of the day, she got a call from Mumbai. Mohan's call at that unusual office time made her worried to begin with.

Mohan, in a stern and concerned voice, related to her that her father, Yeshwant, was seriously ailing and needed to be hospitalised.

Shalini got nervous, jittered. In an already mentally weak state, just in a flash, all ugly and corrupt thoughts ran through her mind. Mind is the slave of the situation and environment around you. It takes no time to start feeling the way the environment around you treats you. Two days of stress, negativity, and despair made her mind start thinking of all, the worst first.

At the same time, she gathered herself quickly. Though Yeshwant needed urgent medical attention and carved a new sector of worries for her, Shalini, for once also felt relieved to get her mind a break from the project shackles for some time. Not that the break was pleasant, but a break all right. As she was readying to break free briefly from one set of fetters, another was readying to greet her with open arms. Venkat and Murali took over the perils and reassured her to leave.

She rushed home, grabbed a few apparels as she could grope from her wardrobe, piled them in a streetcar bag, and dialled Santosh. He made a quick flight booking for her and within no time, Shalini was off to the Kempegowda Airport to reach Mumbai. She luckily weathered the Bengaluru Road traffic and reached the airport in time. On her way in the cab, she made a quick call, first to Devayani, her mother and then to Shweta. Devayani was puzzled, shaking, and uncontrollably sobbing. One of the next-lane neighbours and Shalini's cousin, Mohan, had arrived in no time, and had taken Yashwant to the nearest multi-speciality hospital. Yashwant was admitted to the ICU. Devayani was sitting outside, wondering what would happen next.

Shalini said," Aai, do not worry, Baba will be fine. I have left from here, about to catch the flight and should be reaching in the next couple of hours. What are the doctors saying?" Devayani was faintly aware of what exactly Yashwant was going through, but too stressed out, so she summoned her nephew and handed over the phone to him. Mohan informed Shalini, "stroke."

Yashwant was brought in fast, and hence major complications were evaded, but Yashwant's age and the severity of the stroke were likely to throw up several challenges. Yashwant was under observation in the ICU and continued to stay perilous.

Shalini informed Mohan about her flight schedule and almost pleaded with him to take care of his aunt till she arrived. She and Mohan were childhood buddies and dependable pals, but Shalini became formal with him, as she rendered herself utterly helpless and flabbergasted. But with Mohan around, she was at least not worried about her mother. Mohan assured her to stay calm and not to worry for his uncle and aunt. That gave Shalini some respite in her transit.

She then dialled Shweta. Shweta was already informed by Devayani, and she was frantically trying to call Shalini to check her whereabouts. As Shalini got Shweta online, both sighed in relief. Shweta was equally concerned about her father's well-being. She, though being younger of the siblings, was deeply saddened and concerned by the turn of events.

Siya had her board exams from the day after, and Shweta had to stay back in Delhi for her. She relayed her leave of absence to Shalini and assured her to be in touch for anything Shalini needed. Shweta's nature always propelled her to withdraw from responsibilities and assume an easy position. Her being junior in the family made this easy for her nature. That always made Shalini accountable, answerable, and in charge. Shalini, for once, felt Shweta shrugged off again, but as she expanded her mind space, she realised the seriousness of Siya's exams and handed over the benefit of doubt to Shweta, at least that time around. She once again assumed her elderhood and took the onus upon herself.

Shalini was restless after she finished the security check. Till then, check-in and other formalities kept her busy. She realised she was so famished that she could even eat a horse. She thought that first eating a stomach full would mean she would have lost the severity of her father's critical condition. She was not getting ready to dine, wanted to keep her pain only to keep her aware and conscious about what her family was going through. She could not wipe the echo off of the sobbing noise of her mother, she heard on the phone, and it was melting her heart out. She wanted to refrain from anything that would make her comfortable and seemingly content. She wanted herself to be stoic as if it were her distant support and contribution to the trauma her family was going through far away. During that emotional surrender, Santosh called her to check if all was in line and she succumbed to the circumstances and let go her emotions off. He counseled her well, assured her to be speaking to Mohan and ordered her to get herself dined before she boarded. The spat they had just a day back, had got quelled, albeit by an undesired reason.

As if Santosh was the reason to dilute her guilt, Shalini agreed with herself to dine and satiate her screaming hunger. Shalini came to the rational discretion zone, chose her favourite menu platter and ate it fast and well. Food in her empty stomach made her feel far better than she was, wanting and yearning, some time back.

In some time, she boarded the plane and dozed off in no time. She was tired, tuckered out, first due to Murugan and then due to Yeshwant and his collapse. She had been battling nerves since the previous day. She slept like a rock only to be awakened by the thud of the aircraft landing. It was an Airbus A320. 'Not a smooth landing,' she exclaimed to herself.

'If nothing is smooth, why should the landing be different?,' the sardonic thought took her control.

The plane took a long taxi and reached the aerobridge after almost ten minutes of landing. As the aerobridge abutted the plane and the doors were about to open, Shalini tried to rush to the exit, feeling she should be excused and made way for, as she rode an emergency. As she rushed through the aisle a couple of rows ahead, the passengers nearer to the exit already risen by then, were bustling to get their cabin baggages off the overhead luggage compartments and stood to block the aisle. She felt barricaded and restless, but soon realised that she might need a long walk to the arrivals, perhaps a quick drop at the restroom and fetch a taxi. Hence, rushing and pushing then was of little use. She waited a couple of rows ahead and eventually disembarked the plane in the next few minutes. She gathered herself, quickly clubbed her curls and tresses in her left hand and bound them up in a barrette. An Associate Director, otherwise, looks then were the last thing on her mind. She collected her poise and started her walk, with long strides, lugging her trolley bag, stuffed with clothes that randomly came to her hand, to the arrival and exit. On reaching the arrival, her accumulated edginess, suddenly found a thrust, and she almost ran to the taxi stand.

It wasn't late in the night, while she managed to get herself a taxi. As her taxi merged on the Western Express Highway, she could see a sea of cars with crimson red tail lamps all over the road. 'Welcome to Mumbai,' she thought. She had undergone one ordeal in Bengaluru earlier in the day. The sequel was shot in Mumbai. She had dialled Devayani to inform her that she was approaching the hospital as soon as she hopped into the taxi. But it was well past an hour later that she reached the hospital gate.

The visiting hours were closed long ago, but she managed to squeeze through the security. Very often in a traumatic mindset, one miraculously gains some divine strength and coercive skills to win over bureaucratic boundaries. Shalini too acquired that situation-driven esoteric dexterity and reached the fifth floor ICU, where she first caught sight of Mohan, who was standing with folded hands, resting against a wall. As he picked her sight, he inched towards her. She approached him briefly, and she mumbled, "Mohan, what are they saying?" She just rested her head on Mohan's right shoulder as she enquired.

Mohan gave her the update. Yeshwant was out of danger.

"Kaka isn't staring at the immediate threat. He is seriously critical but stable," Mohan echoed these words to Shalini. He further added that Yeshwant had his right side paralysed and would need attention to cure. Shalini got a bit eased out on hearing this. She was happy to hear that her father had some more time left. When she got the call from Mohan earlier in the day, she was expecting the worst, and that psyched her from within. Hope was only to follow her initial despair, but much later. And now, she was much better, though she foresaw far too many challenges in store. She quizzed where her mother was, and ran to her with open arms as she spotted her. Both let some precious tears off, but the latest update from the ICU had given them both, a solace, at least for the time being.

Shalini could not see her father in the ICU as it was late at night. The security down could have been kind or gullible, but the fifth-floor guards did not budge an inch. She sat for a while and decided to proceed to their home, along with Devayani. Mohan extended his courtesy to stay back for his uncle overnight, and let the passage for Shalini, who had such an eventful day, to the home at Goregaon. Hitherto, Yeshwant's being out of immediate danger was a silver lining to the stormy day she had experienced. Both hopped into a taxi and started to find their way out to their home.

Shalini kept thinking. She was frustrated same time, last night, wanted to quit her job, and spent some time to collect herself and think ahead. But almost like a mechanical robot, she rose in the morning, got herself ready, manoeuvred through the traffic, got the stick in the meeting, gulped in some late lunch, only to be called for her father's emergency, and had gotten physically and mentally ready all over.

Ever since she got her cousin's call, she had totally forgotten the annoyances she had undergone over her project since the previous day. One torment completely took over another in no time.

Shalini reached her maternal home around midnight. She slept by her mother, and within no time, she caught the rapid eye movement of sleep. She might have encountered several dreams, quite a few which would make one restless when awake, but by the time she woke up the next day, she had no memory of any. She did not have a sound sleep either.

She finished her morning rituals and phoned Mohan. Mohan was supposed to be relieved of his vigil services, and she quickly sipped a cup of tea, dunked herself with some warm water as if to call it a bath, and left for the hospital to free her cousin, who not only brought her father to the hospital on time, but showed the kind heart to stay put at the ICU, derived from the warmth and love of the childhood camaraderie and his love and affection for his uncle.

Shalini reached the hospital, schemed through the entry procedures, and reached the ICU floor. Mohan was waiting for her. There was no deterioration in Yeshwant's condition, which were signs of encouragement. Shalini was along with her laptop, as she knew the kind-heartedness of her project team would not survive her medical emergency for too long. Shalini anticipated another long day, testing her patience and endurance.

She was now optimistically hopeful that her father would go back home in a few days, but was disconcerted by the thoughts of how he would be managed in a paralytic condition at home. Steeped in these thoughts, she peeped at the laptop screen and started to respond to her emails. And the number of unread emails made her heart thaw. 123 unread emails ever since she fled from the office in the afternoon the previous day! 'Such a muck I am in,' Shalini protested to herself.

As she was scrolling her screen down, the previous day stood firmly before her. Within a flash, the turn of events ran through her, from Murugan's cross-bossism, to the heart wrenching call about Yeshwant's health, to Santosh's booking her the flight, forgetting the scuffle they had on Sunday, her unending travel from the airport to the hospital, the denial of entry to the ICU to at least glance at her ailing father and finally reaching her old home at Goregaon, with Devayani.

As she had reached her maternal home, she had some sense of weird nostalgia. The home was her own, where she grew in her formative years, yet it appeared to her as a stranger's house. As Shaunak grew, she could visit here only once a year, sometimes even less frequently.

She quickly recollected her time with Yeshwant and Devayani, and her fights with Shweta. The house was the same, only that it had fewer occupants then. The furniture hadn't changed much. The bookshelf was the same, books more tattered than how she had left them, the kitchen was the same, with that familiar odour of the house still prevalent.

Yeshwant had come to Goregaon in the mid-80s with Devayani and their small daughter. A diligent banker, he got transferred from his last posting at Nasik. Though Shalini was born in Nasik, she was reared in Mumbai and identified herself as a Mumbaikar. Her upbringing was around middle-class values, and her parents lived those values for their daughters to follow them effortlessly. Shweta was born in Goregaon and always deemed herself a more Mumbaikar than her elder sister.

Shalini was a good student, and so was Shweta. She kept her academics well ahead of other matters and earned a fame and distinction of being a focused, obedient, approachable, and compassionate among the Purohit siblings. She had secured admission to Noble Institute, one of the most sought-after engineering colleges in Mumbai, purely on her merit. The wheat-complexioned Shalini traversed her engineering in electronics very fluently and completed her master's in wireless communication networks. She was picked up on the campus and offered a position with a renowned software giant, *Xtusu*. It was since then that she had built her journey and career in the software industry, as she had reached the position she was in by then, although she needed a couple of changes in between, in the twenty-five-odd years of her service. In her present job, her association with Murugan was only two years old.

Shweta, on the other hand, was a much-happening soul. She made the Purohit's house a potboiler and kept the vibrancy in the house on its toes. She was multifaceted, enjoyed dance and music and kept her academic progress going with equal poise. As it is almost always schemed, two siblings of the same house were poles apart in likes, tastes, and preferences. Shweta chose the medical side and pursued her dentistry, with advanced specialisation later.

As Shalini and Shweta both reached the marriage age one after the other, Yeshwant had become a senior banker and wore a high designation. He was ready to get both his daughters married, with fanfare and conforming to the societal expectations. A father of two daughters, he was mindful of his responsibilities and led a constrained life to ensure his daughters ended up with a good education and, eventually, good in-laws.

Devayani, on the other hand, prided being the wife of a senior banker, wore the lifestyle that suited such a wife. Converse to Yeshwant, the mother of two daughters, one of them more ardent and enthusiastic than the other, she lived her life flamboyantly, but measuredly, and was a jolly, caring and friendly mother of two.

As both daughters had left the home, neither of the parents had the keen interest as they previously had, to keep their house up-to-date, modern and adorned. Shalini found the house was not in a mess, tidy and kept as it always was, but lacked a modern, contemporary look, fewer in gadgets and appliances. Afterall, since both the daughters distanced a thousand kilometers from them each, the parents did not augur their frequent coming and were happy to stay with their middling, old lifestyle.

Shalini rolled through all the memories as she steadied herself over the laptop screen, in the vicinity of the ICU. She realised that the drawing room of the Goregaon home needed a makeover; the paint could not be identified with what the original shade was when applied a decade or two back. She juxtaposed this with her drawing room in her Malleswaram apartment. It was state-of-the-art, well-lit with ornamental light fittings, adequately and modularly furnished. For once, she thought her parents deserved better. 'But all this, if and after Yeshwant held his health well,' she said to herself. She came back from the journey of thoughts and memories to the real world, where her father was ailing, supposedly out of danger, but battling a stroke and complications of age.

She realised she was torn between work and home, parents and her small family and good and bad thoughts. She realised she had not called home to check Santosh's or Shaunak's whereabouts. She had the last call with Santosh well past midnight the previous day, and had expressed her momentary relief to him about Yeshwant's health. Shaunak was to speak to her that morning, but neither she could ring him nor had he buzzed her so far. It was 9:30 in the morning. 'The prince would be in his ornamental palace now,' she quipped to herself. She thought of buying some time to connect with Shaunak.

The unread emails kept piling. She could not focus at all and shut the laptop screen to let it sleep. She walked to the nurses' counter and enquired when she could meet the doctor. The doctor was expected at 11:00. She returned to her provisional workstation, but not to work. She glanced at her phone and decided to call Shaunak. She was walking a tight rope, managing her mother, caring for her father, keeping company with her husband, worrying for her son, and trying to solve the mess in her office she had gotten into.

Shaunak answered her call within a couple of rings. He was concerned about his mother and his grandfather. As he was updated late previous night by his father, Shaunak had lesser determination to call his mother and enquire her wellbeing, first up. He was content that matter was still under control. So, as he picked Shalini's call, he muttered," Mamma, good to know that Ajoba is stable and out of danger." Shalini was relieved to know Shaunak was in tune and belonged to the circumstances.

Shalini however pressed, "Shaunu, though Ajoba is stable, and not as critical as he was, he stares at bigger problems, as and if he returns home. He is paralyzed on the right, and will need continuous help and support even for his daily chores. Aaji will not be able to manage him all by herself and we are not sure how long it will take to recover, even if he does. I will be required to stay here for a few more days, even a couple of weeks. Keep company to your father and let him feel he has a son who is grown up now and an able shoulder to rely upon in such cases of exigency."

Shaunak responded maturely "No worries, Mamma, we shall make some way out to take care of Ajoba as he comes back."

Amidst the onslaught she underwent for the last two days, she was hell relieved by Shaunak's assuaging words. For once, she felt her son had perhaps grown.

Santosh

As he spoke with Shalini and had asked her to dine well, Santosh had reached home by that time. He was sipping over a coffee and had dialled Mohan.

Santosh queried pensively, “Mohan, Hi. How are things there? Shalini has left, and she should reach there by nine. What are the doctors hinting?”

Mohan informed him of the update, which gave Santosh a respite. Yeshwant had a few more nights in store, if not too many. He was relieved that the ultimate sad moment was not at the doorstep. He was sheepishly calmed by the thought that he would not be needed to fly to Mumbai immediately. He took big gulps of the coffee that had grown warmer by then. Though his father-in-law was in no immediate danger, Mohan’s tone did not send him a comforting signal either. He was thoughtfully staring at his coffee, which was growing colder by each passing moment. Thoughts galloped one after the other. From Shalini’s state of mind, not able to cope with her work, to Shaunak’s future, to this newly thrust challenge. For a moment, he got worried about his parents too, who could be stricken with health issues at any time, given their ages. Shalini atleast has Shweta to look upto, but he felt all by himself if such a calamity should have arisen.

Battling the swirls of thoughts, Santosh bottomed the coffee and got up. He thought of cooking some quick stuff, reheating the morning leftover and setting up a quick dinner.

He was a simple but purposeful man with less specific penchants in life. A family man, one can say. But when it came to office and his career, he was a tiger. His growth had been phenomenal and fast-tracked. He was one of the youngest directors in his organisation. Santosh was gifted the knack of excellent time management. He always seemed to have more time at his disposal, and he made the completion of tasks and activities look haplessly easy. That is where the real challenges started. His team would never be able to match his pace and tread and he would often need to face this dichotomy. He would frequently expect his members to match him, and overestimated their capabilities comparing with his. This led to friction and abrasions. He was not a hateful personality in the office, but people were uncomfortable with him, due to his ability to handle super efforts easily. His supreme talent and ability, however, always scored over these pitfalls, and he remained one of the fastest achievers of his company, for many years in a row.

Santosh, too, carried a value system that was born out of a middle-class upbringing. He was waiting for Shaunak to company him for the night's dinner. With that hope, he rang Shaunak to check his schedule. He knew his adolescent kid had only late entries to home. He dialled in the hope that the gravity of the family event could coincidentally turn his feet to the home early, that day. But Santosh could not get his son online, for long. He left a text note for his pampered kid to dial him back. Soon, Santosh had admittedly reconciled that he would be dining alone that night.

He scrambled to the kitchen, glanced over the leftovers, some salad volunteers and quickly filled his plate to make it dressier, though it remained humble and mediocre. Santosh loved his food; taste mattered to him, but that day became an exception. He munched the contents of his plate, only as if to finish them off. He wrapped up the table top, mopped a few stains and slid the plates and cutlery into the kitchen sink. He quickly praised himself for a neat job even in that sombre mood and hung in the wait to receive a call back from his son.

As he inched to his bar, his phone rang, and his dear son was calling to complete his pending task. Santosh grabbed his phone, and as if to remind himself that he fathered his son, answered in a grave, firm tone to start the conversation.

Shaunak was taken aback to have missed his father's calls, and as he rationalised his thoughts, he was curious to know why Santosh called him, which he did very occasionally. He mercifully pleaded with his father, "Dad, I had a flat tyre, my mobile battery had conked off, and I could get your message just now. What's up?"

Santosh has no reason to disbelieve his son and calmly disposed, retaining his paternal stoic tone, as if sounding to his son, about his earlier misdeed of missing his call. He related, in a sound voice," Shaunak, Yeshwant Ajoba is hospitalised, and Mamma has flown to Mumbai earlier this evening. I was waiting for you to dine, and now I just finished mine. When are you back home?"

Shaunak got flummoxed on listening to this. He was a bit nervous, but perhaps only just. As a child, he had not spent too much time with the older Purohits. Like grandkids who are very fond of their grandparents, who fondle and cuddle the kids, Shaunak had little memories with the older generations, despite being the first grandchild of the family. That Shalini and Santosh moved out very early in their careers kept the grandchild away from the close warmth of the grandparents. Their being busy in their careers and distance apart kept that association further smeared.

But Shaunak felt for his mother and his dad, who was waiting for him to be back home to share some time in this distress. His not responding in time to his father made him a bit embarrassed.

"Dad, Hope he is good, leaving from here and should be home in fifteen." Shaunak hung up.

Santosh believed Yashwant was mostly not in danger of life anymore. He just wanted his son to be around him, on that lonely evening. He was pleased from within that it was only a quarter of an hour, at best a half, that would smash his solitude. Man is strong, but needs a company to stay stronger. He opened his bar and pulled out the Texan home crafted Vodka bottle, sitting gracefully in the company of single malts and exquisite wines. He was referred to that vodka by his colleagues during his last visit to the US, and he got it jacked on his way back.

Santosh, though he had less penchants, was a connoisseur of food and drinks. He remained intrigued and fond of collecting exotic liquor and drinks. He relished the delectable foods of any cuisine and enjoyed his food at each meal. That he had a mellowed version on his plate that evening was a serious climb down. As if he pitied himself for this, he wanted his son around, and in his absence, moved to his bottle and the chalice, to company him thus.

Late into the night, Santosh had called Shalini to enquire about the hospital update. He was relieved to learn the status quo. Just before, Shaunak also had returned home and had learnt the earlier update from his father.

Santosh had spent some select moments of conversation with Shaunak as he arrived. Such conversations between the father and the son did not last for more than a few minutes. Either of them was inclined to wrap up the conversation, not because they wanted to, but because they could not think and keep the conversation going beyond those minutes. Strange that Shaunak could chat the whole day with the Tushars, Sayonas and other friends, and Santosh could deliver a two-hour project update incessantly, but when it came to chatting with each other, they found themselves seriously short of words and expressions. Fortunately, the father-son duo understood the lines between their silence, and never insisted upon each other to express themselves more, though they would have surely felt happier even if either of them did. Verbosity came to stay with Shalini when it concerned her son.

As Shaunak lunged into his room and got his headset to his ears, Santosh went ahead to search his pending pleasure in the glass. The glass got filled, once again, with the crystal white vodka, this time with some slices of lemon, which Santosh had purposely and thoughtfully kept aside during his dinner cooking encounter. It was such an innocuous act, but it gave just quick evidence of

Santosh's planning skills and why he got things done in quick time, compared to others.

Santosh dug himself into a novel, as he emptied his glass, only to please himself that he read something before going to bed. He might not have even read a couple of paragraphs in, when he would have realised he was snoring.

Santosh got up, as usual, in the morning and got ready for the routine daily grind, more today, to get the update from Mumbai. He thought not to tinkle Shalini so early in the morning and waited for her to settle in before he conversed with her.

So, he continued with his chores. Yogini had arrived by then and got updated on Shalini's absence and the need to extend more help, thus. She readied for the cooking session and even helped to get the kitchen clean. She brought to the notice of the man in charge of the home that the clothes from the washing machine were not out for drying and volunteered herself to win some brownie points in the unsettled times for the Upadhyayas.

Santosh was not well placed after his father-in-law's sudden downfall and wife's absence, and decided to take that pause to reach the office late. His sluggish and occasionally confused movements mirrored his intent. He spent more time than usual on the newspapers and had his second round of tea. He rarely gets the chance to have a second tea round at home, on work days.

Those days, with late-night sleep and stress, as it came without invitation, Santosh often confronted acidity. He was proud that he could handle late nights and early morning flight departures with ease, but this belief was getting gradually but increasingly shattered. Not that he had grown old enough to get embraced by those fringe embellishments, but the weight of performances, self-induced pressures, unexpressed anxiety for the son, all kept taking a toll on him, not to a worrying level, but one that certainly disposed him from his old carefree, immune version. His HbA1c bordered on the pre-diabetic levels, and his lipid profile did not send smiles. Yet Santosh, with the zeal and drive of the habitual work-life equation, kept his chin high and back straight. His sideburns, however, had begun to grow grey, and he had started to feel balder than before.

He heard Shaunak murmur in his room and believed that the mom-son conversation was underway. He liked his son's dialogue with Shalini as he himself could never get engaged in such prolonged conversations with Shaunak. Shalini invariably was his mediator and he kept learning about the insights of Shaunak, mostly through that arrangement.

When he was a child, Santosh was quite shy, mixed little with kids his age and had very few friends. His childhood was not a troubled one, but he did not enjoy a very cheerful and happening one either. He was hardworking, reflective but was very poor at accosting and befriending. Later, as he gained glory, fame, and money, he became a vastly improved version of his childhood, but this tendency did creep in at times and he would go into his own cocoon.

Yeshwant's event rekindled that tendency of his, and he went inwards. Such inward movement kept him less popular among his colleagues, though he never let a chance pass on his quality of work and throughput.

Santosh was uneasy, and wasn't certain why he was. He began to realise that he was getting trapped in his old habit, but he found no force to kick himself out. The Texan Vodka only sugarcoated his situation.

Yogini had prepared the morning and afternoon meals, and Santosh waited for his turn for a late morning breakfast. Yogini cooked well, and she prepared poha. She hailed from Madhya Pradesh, and poha was her delectable delicacy. She, in most probability, caught Santosh pensive and had cooked him is favorite breakfast dish. As she had entered the home, she was already briefed about Yeshwant's condition and Shalini's absence. She empathised with the situation and put her best foot forward to calm the nerves of the Upadhayay family, with her contribution. The food lover of the house, who had to be content with an ordinary meal last evening, had something to cheer over the impending meal.

Yogini spoke chaste Hindi and had come along with her husband Govind, many years ago in Bengaluru. Govind was a site supervisor and had been employed for a very large construction site, in the outskirts of the city, through a labour contractor of Indore origins. That brought him there, and he had become fond of the city to extend his home there. He got site calls, earned well then, but also got served with periods of lull when Yogini, with her steady flow of money, kept the ball rolling. They both were yet to be blessed with a child, but did not give up hope. They avoided too much strenuous efforts on costly affairs like the IVF despite being urged by some fellow mates. In fact, they realised they would not be able to afford it so easily, and kept putting in the conventional efforts with optimism. In moments of despair, Govind reiterated his desire to go back to Indore, but Yogini somehow kept him intact and pressed forward her steady income to his solace. Yogini was dear to a few homes like that of the Upadhyayas, who delivered her and Govind the comfort to press through daunting times too.

Santosh, despite getting tangled in his web of intermittent diffidence, was a presentable and courteous gentleman. Yogini never felt uneasy with even just Santosh around in the house, which was usually rare, though.

As she wrapped up all her chores, she signalled Santosh about it, and she left the home. The house was left all for the Upadhyaya men once again.

Santosh relished his favourite breakfast, and for a change, had his junior on the table, who had tastes diagonal to his father. Honouring the situation, Shaunak reluctantly gulped just about half a plateful of Poha, leaving some around the dish on the table and some in the dish. He knew the house help, Swati, would get it all cleaned up later. He picked a handful of cut fruits and bottomed up his glass of milk, to leave for another happening day.

Santosh sauntered around the house and showed no signs to hurry up. But he soon realised the backlog of emails and meetings that would be hounding him as he would reach office. He gathered all that he could from the dining table, flung it in the kitchen sink and pressed forward to be ready for his encounter in the office.

As he reversed his car from the parking, he was immersed in his thoughts of the past. He got on the driveway and then took the long march to the exit gate.

Santosh, when he was seven, had an accidental fall into a well. His mother, Yashoda, hailed from a beautiful town in Konkan, *Pavas*. Lush green, with sea at a stone's throw away, his maternal abode was a heavenly habitat.

It was during those years that Santosh had gone for a vacation. His maternal cousins flocked there regularly over school holidays, and it was Santosh's first time being there. His father, Madhusudan, was a banker in a central bank and had several postings away from Mumbai, even outside Maharashtra. That kept Yashoda and Santosh away from his maternal abode. That year, they both had made it and were planned to be escorted back by Madhusudan as they would wrap up their stay.

Despite being not fully gelled with his cousins, on one such day, Santosh went with them for an afternoon holiday affair, from aimless roaming in the *wadis;* small farmyards studded with coconut, betelnut, cashew, and mango trees, to kite flying on the nearby sea shore and water fun in the family well.

Santosh could not swim, but not being able to swim would not have mattered much, as the well, as big and deep as it was, was well crafted with steps to climb down and immerse the feet in, and safely and gleefully accept splashes of water thrown at, as one sat on them.

All his other cousins were frogs in the well, jumping and pumping so adeptly. Santosh had steadied himself, two steps above the water level and continued to watch his pals enjoy the water experience.

The steps of the well weren't broad but neither narrow enough to let a person slip off balance. But Santosh did. Without knowing why and what happened, he found himself with water around, faintly able to hear his cousins giggling over the top. It took a moment or two for the cousins, who were otherwise busy hushing and pushing each other, to realise that Santosh had 'tasted' the deep waters.

Santosh must have dived down at least five to six feet before physics brought him up to the surface. At the first sight of the sky, he gasped for breath. He was terrified by that close encounter, which could not keep him still. He went down again, and the place where he had propped up was reduced to bubbles. By then, Dushant, his maternal cousin who was luckily older than him, had held him by his arm and pulled him up. Two more from the coterie came close and lifted him to help him grab a mouthful of air. Santosh started howling loudly, which made a few elders run to the scene of the act.

The gang of water enthusiasts, with a few elders, brought Santosh up on the ground. He had ingested a good amount of water, but not so much to be concerned. The scars of the underwater ordeal and loss of breath made him psyched. Yashoda had come running by then, only to find her son safe, but not before undergoing a tumultuous adventure.

As he was ending the driveway to the exit gate, he encountered a dog suddenly crossing his way, and he applied his brakes with utmost purpose, just as the car missed the dog by a whisker. A few meters of the driveway were painted black by the scraping tyres who were ordered to stop against the wish of the engine and even theirs, as if a mark of protest. Santosh had his heart in his mouth as he almost relived the past encounter in the well.

'Not a good start to a morose day,' he spoke to himself.

Shalini

Not able to concentrate on her work and still anxious to wait for the doctor, Shalini just sat on the bench outside the ICU. She was waiting for the visiting hours to allow her see her ailing father, tapping her feet anxiously in the wait. At the stroke of ten, she rushed to the ICU security guard and earned her entry to the ICU.

Bed No. 15 wore the name of Yeshwant Purohit. She reached to the right side of the bed. The bed had multiple monitors around to adorn it, and a few of them would send periodic beeps as if to remind of the intensity of the situation. Yeshwant was sleeping with his eyes closed. His face looked pale, his body appeared frail, and he lay there listless. Out of anxious curiosity, Shalini asked the ward nurses for any opinion. One of the nurses said with a straight face, "Doctor will update on this."

Shalini could not make sense of that cold and flat statement. She turned back to her father, who showed some signs of movement at the eyelids. She was excited to see him animate, and she looked with hope towards the nurse, who had come to change the IV bottle. The nurse turned to the patient and patted him on his shoulder. Yeswant had decided not to deliver more at that juncture.

Shalini caressed the forehead of her father, ran her fingers through his silver-grey hair, and let out a suppressed whimper. Yeshwant was tall, around 5'8", weak as that age would offer to his health, with a long face, and thick grey eyebrows, which might have been dark in his younger days. His cheekbones were almost seen from a distance, and his white beard stubble covered his face. He would have been quite handsome in his wee days.

Shalini was trying to decipher what that nurse could have meant. Either she was not qualified to relay the diagnosis, or she wanted to remain euphemistic in narrating the truth and hence avoided the conversation. Shalini feared for the latter. As if a penance for her of being not with her father in those difficult moments, she stood near the ICU bed, just to register her presence.

Only that long, till she was told by the nurse to stay outside the ward. An ICU ward is an unpleasant eyesore with several patients seen battling critical illnesses, some moaning gruesomely, some languid and battling for their lives. Unless for a qualified and trained medical professional or a paramedic, staying in that ward for too long is a test of mental strength. So, the nurse had rightfully advised Shalini to wait outside unless she was paged for intervention.

Shalini glanced at her father once again, before she proceeded to the exit. She dragged herself out and grabbed her seat again.

"Santosh, I just went and saw Baba inside the ICU. He was lying still, motionless. I could not watch him anymore. Doctors will come after 11:00 am, and I will get a further update. But there seems to be no change from the situation of last night," Shalini rang up Santosh and expressed to him.

"Let us wait for the doctors. And whatever the update, I am there with you and Aai. Let me know if I need to be there, and I will fly immediately" Santosh reassured her.

They went on to talk for a while, some contemplatively intimate, all things which a wife under duress would share with her husband on a remote access, till Santosh reached his office parking and needed to take the elevator. Their conversation thus ended.

Shalini reopened the laptop screen and began to scan through the emails, just in case to pick something urgent. After a marathon Sunday and the previous day, she was spared from anything dire, and she sighed as she shut the screen off.

Sometime later, by noon, she had an encounter with the doctor, and the doctor apprised her that Yeshwant was out of danger, and would come to his senses soon, but he would have his right side totally ineffective and would need continuous paramedic support even at home to take care of his basic needs. Given his age, his right side would crawl back sluggishly to normalcy, and even that would be numbered in months. She, at that moment, wished Santosh were by her side.

By that time, Devayani was up there, and she was too relieved by the verdict but perturbed by the challenges in store.

Shalini also dialled Mohan to update him on all the latest findings and thanked him once again for his timely help.

That her father was safe now removed the fifty-ton load from her head. She got a bit relieved but equally fraught by the future contests at home.

Yeshwant got discharged after a stay of eleven days. From the day when Shalini anxiously waited for the doctor to pronounce the findings, to the date of discharge, Yeshwant was getting better, only by inches. When the hospital was convinced that there was no further role for them to treat him, they accepted the request for discharge, which had started to gain clamour from the seventh day.

Shalini had been away from the office for a week. During that time, riding on a weekend, Santosh made a quick visit to Mumbai and improved his score as a son-in-law. Purohits did not have a son, so Santosh, being their elder son-in-law, doubled as an occasional son too. Both Yeshwant and Devayani had pampered him in his early marriage days.

Shalini wasn't adding to improve the situation there, which wasn't as desperate as it was earlier, but her helplessness made her antsy. Not that she was not away from the office for long in the past, but each time such a fortnightly absence was reserved for long vacations, which were fun-filled and refreshing. This long break was no uplifting in any measure.

She started lobbying for his discharge once Yeshwant's condition stabilised beyond further degeneration. She knew she was pressing for his exit from the hospital, only to be confronted with a bigger role and handling at their Goregaon abode, but she wanted to purchase some change.

Change! She had a hankering for, for the last many years. At the office, no little change she could make off late, Shaunak wasn't aligned to change and gather so quickly anytime soon, and hence she started to try her hand at something to *change*, as out of context it could be, at least the bed and place for her father.

She was feeling trapped and had no place to escape. Shweta spoke to her and Devayani, thrice a day, but her not being there made Shalini 'The face of the rescue act.'

She sincerely wished Shweta to come and share her burden, both physically and mentally. Besides, Devayani, at her age, flung all the frontline challenges at Shalini and could only best stay concerned, troubled and dependent.

Shalini wanted to escape, but was completely ensnared. She wanted to escape from the unwanted frills of her father's health hazard, from the worries of her son and his future, the over-dependability of her mother on her, the turmoil she underwent in her office now and then, her bodily changes and accompanying those, some pains, and discredits. She was grilled a sandwich.

Shaunak

A little disturbed by the turn of events in the Purohit family, Shaunak was not left in the best of his moods.

His graduation was nearing its end. He, for moments, used to feel that he was going nowhere. A 'B. Com degree', could be higher second class at best, and then what?' he freaked at times. His pending work at college, which would barricade his already mediocre academic progress, kept him jittery. He was searching for a purpose, a direction, and an intent.

He took regular turns at fun in all that kids of his age would normally be engaged in. Sometimes, some blurred moments of infatuation would grab his mind, but to whom, he was not able to arrive at.

The age which just transcends the teen is the captivating chase behind a target, which is on a constant move. Very often, such targets are mirages.

What is a mirage, and what a rainbow is? They exist, it appears to be, they seem to be, yet they do not! It is all an expansion of imagination, but the mind gnawingly gets deceived into this. This expansion is the identification with that unreal world, that is, its illusory awareness. In it, one unknowingly dunks the feet in; Shaunak, Shalini Santosh, Devayani, you, me, he, she, all alike... It is momentary, fickle, uncertain, even if expressed... yet the feet remain completely dry.

Shaunak was not sure if he wanted to get drenched per se, but hitherto, he remained totally dry. He wanted to search, but he could not figure out what he wanted to. He was gripped by something which he could not comprehend, express and was ineffable for him.

Not Shaunak alone, but all of us, living or non-living beings, are bound by the three gunas of the universe. Each being, living or non-living, is influenced by the three gunas: *Sattva*, *Rajas* and *Tamas*. Whereas *Sattva*'s dominance takes one to spiritualism, righteousness and inner peace, *Rajas* brings in desires and ambitions. The *Tamas* guna is the one which adorns the personality with extreme feelings, including sloth, indifference, and hatred. At any given time, the three gunas reside in a soul or a being, and each guna competes with the other two, as one of the three gains prominence. This tug of war continues as long as 'The being' is alive and kicking.

Shaunak's that phase of life was being dominated by *Tamas*, and *Rajas*, and whenever *Sattva* even tried to gain supremacy, *Tamas*, and *Rajas*, more so the *Tamas*, gained strength to retreat him back.

Shaunak was sandwiched between the gunas and their interplay. Age, experience, and earnest efforts to achieve, along with the establishment of pure vibes, were the factors which would have gradually taken his course to his destiny. But that would have been a factor of time.

He was struggling to exert effort to scale his path. He occasionally wanted to, but the prevalence and predominance of the activated *Tamas* guna always dragged him backwards.

He was aware that his mother wanted him to perform, travel abroad for higher studies, his father perhaps too. Not that he detested that situation, but he was terrified of the efforts, responsibility he would have to wear to get him there.

Shaunak was a cameoed piece of luck, who fell gently in the cushion of the Upadhyay couple and was fondly caressed, as if the only precious possession. That possession was also entrusted with a sense of ownership, askance. The parents lived the dream of his success so closely that it bogged down the easy-going, happy-go-lucky charming young man, who was aimless and clueless, with burdened confusion tantamount to his age and stage of life.

In the vibrant, bowling age, where the gunas are in special random motion, Shaunak had a task at hand, without his knowledge.

Shaunak rose from the dining chair, as if commanded to go for a bath. He was not sure he wanted to bathe and leave for college. At college, the assignments pending, he wanted to turn away from the professor's wrath, and more from the slide of the GPA, lest he not make a meaningful conclusion of his commerce attempt.

He tried to pucker his earnest efforts far too many times, with this gathered realisation, and the fact he could not deliver the punch would make him nervous and dejected.

With thoughts galore, he left home and rode to his college without a pit stop at *the Fromer's*. As he reached his college, his professor gave him a stern earful and he was embarrassed, especially when a handful of those, whom he got occasionally drawn into and momentarily infatuated with were witnesses to his humiliation.

He had a little idea that Sayona fell for him, and as at least she was not around, made him sigh in ease. She came from a rich family, the Mehras, who had a car dealership of one of the largest auto makers. She was the younger of the two siblings and drew utmost care and affection from the Mehra couple. The Mehras had been in the car business for over two generations. Harmeet

Singh, Sayona's grandfather, started his flirtation with the car business in Jalandhar, and his son grew and steadied the foothold. They settled in Bhopal for the last two decades, and Sayona shifted all the way from Bhopal to Bengaluru to bump into Shaunak and her tryst with Mass Communications.

She was fair, slender, dark-eyed, with silky hair, and wore a sharp nose on her prettily crafted oval face. Her thick, black, pruned eyebrows added charm to her fair complexion, and the overall package made an involuntary appeal. That Shaunak sometimes felt something for her was not for nothing. She earnestly wanted Shaunak to be attracted to her. He sent her the right signals, only just, even unintentionally, for her to remain interested.

She was always exquisitely dressed around a model-like figure. That whole day, Shaunak's encounter with his tutor made her miss meeting him and she missed him thoroughly. His absence at *the Fromer's* also made her nervous.

By night, not able to stand away, she dialled Shaunak. He was in his room, with the high-quality headset around his ears. He at first could not pick the phone ringing, as his ear gear was engulfed with too loud hard rock. Only when he accidentally glanced at his mobile screen, did he see the screen flashing and Sayona's name blinking. He had mixed feelings on seeing the phone flash with her name. Firstly, he got uneasy to receive a call from her at that hour and at the same time he was elated from within to have had it. He perhaps had wanted to talk to her.

Sayona and Shaunak chatted for quite a long time on the phone. Not intimate or romantic, but the conversation was heading to break the barriers and draw them closer. The call went longer than what Shaunak had intended to begin with, and with each passing minute, it felt like he wanted it to continue.

Shaunak eventually hung up, lingered in the remberance of the call and tickled his fantasy, felt cuddled from within and rode over that dreamy sequence again. He began to feel that he was falling for Sayona. He shut his eyes and imagined her fair complexion, dark eyes, her chiselled body and felt prickly all over his body. He was feeling happy in that float of ecstasy and cherished each moment he was going through.

"Life is so beautiful," he thought to himself, and "let the beauty unfold more," he quipped. That passage erased all the dichotomy of his mind, brought him clingingly close to the joyous bonds of youth, a gentle, tender, hopeful vigour, and a blooming allure of time. The Love of life, the playful frolics, the blissful courtyard games, the intoxicating fragrance of Jasmine drifted through his body. Without darkness, there in the world, the heart sang in pairs.

Shaunak landed on his senses after a brief hiatus and the dreadful mounts of the onus of excelling in his graduation, readying for a challenging and proof-staking future, much of it weighing over the expectations of his parents made him shudder with shrill. As he started to brood into a pensive, damaging spiral, he also recollected Yeshwant's condition and began to hide behind remorsefulness, having already worn the attire of confusion, desperate inability, and vulnerability.

Shaunak was squeezed between all these, and life had not taught him ways and means to overcome them.

Time was the tool which would have set most of the things right.

Well past midnight, Shaunak had gone into slumber, after a disturbed squiggle in the bed.

Shalini

Yeshwant was home, and a new chapter of struggle had premiered. Shalini had been staying for almost a fortnight now and was desperately waiting for Shweta to relieve her.

As the doctors had predicted, Yeshwant was up for a semi-vegetable state, just about to have gathered senses to respond in a grouchy, husky voice. His paralysed side did not allow him to even turn to the other side while on bed, all by himself. All his activities were confined to the boundaries of his bed.

On the day of discharge, Santosh had come to assist Shailini. As fate would test her more, Mohan had to fly to Lucknow for an important conference and had to absent himself during the discharge ordeal. Santosh gathered the frills of the endeavour and flew down to be by her side.

Her old friends did drop in during that extended hospital stay, but all being in the same stages of their careers, had to refocus on theirs and excused themselves from frequent visits. Also being away from Mumbai kept

Shalini isolated from regular connects and reestablishing it around that tumultuous situation was never going to be easy. Relationship is a function of time, catalysed by sweeter unions. It also applies to friendship, and any sabbatical in either of them only compounds challenges for breaking the ice, anew.

Shalini was still lucky to have earned the empathy and warmth of Mohan, with whom she was very rarely in touch while in Bengaluru. Though she enjoyed and reaped the benefits of her childhood investments, she realised the importance of social connections, which could fetch returns in times of difficulty, especially with friends and contemporaries, not on social media alone, but on a real physical level.

In an already dilapidated state of mind, she invited another challenge of restiveness, feeling lonely and without dependable buddies. She had grown very feeble and delicate from within.

Santosh was the steel support to her, especially with the tete-a-tete in between, and that instilled in her some heavy calories of energy. He ran around to complete all the hospital discharge formalities, bill clearances, to bring Yeshwant to the clear passage of discharge.

Santosh's presence made it easier for Shalini to rest Yeshwant at home. She had already arranged for a caretaker, who was expected to stay with Devyani, round the clock. All was set well, but Yeshwant's condition did not send that comforting solace.

Shalini was riding impatience due to multiple reasons, but the fact that Yeshwant's condition was far from any quick improvement topped that list. She had reassuring conversations with Devayani, just to keep her ageing mother hopeful, but from within she was highly diffident about the future.

The elder son-in-law had flown back a few days ago, and the Goregaon abode of the Purohits had three new guests, Shweta, Arjun and Siya, to join Shalini after her fortnightly solo ordeal.

Shalini wondered that Devayani would collapse into the arms of Shweta at her sight. She would sob inconsolably, and Shweta would gather all the courage to keep her mother good. Shalini lumped in her throat, on the thought of that hyper-emotional scene. But she was extremely taken aback to see her mother and younger sister composed and collected. She at once felt that Shweta should have expressed more emotions at the first sight of her mother, but both were surprisingly quite balanced and collected.

Time blunts the intensity and propensity to react sharply, even during most diabolical instances. Shalini, for once, felt that she had needlessly taken too much toll on herself about the whole event over the last fortnight, as if she were the only one who was at the helm, conferred upon herself all the duties and responsibilities to steer their family ship to safety. Being the elder among the siblings, she took upon herself that Herculean task as if she was the natural, ex-officio custodian of this mission.

She was flummoxed for a few seconds. She started to reminisce about all her one-woman show, right from running to the Bengaluru Airport, being the first to relieve her cousin at the hospital, standing as a rock for her mother, taking all the onus of the turn of events and spending restless hours at the ICU, by a few quarters over-assuming.

She tried to walk into Shweta's shoes. She reached the field after the dust had settled down, after Siya and her family were relieved from the clutches of the board exams, and most importantly, when Devayani had settled down and had begun to sink into the condition of Yeshwant and had perhaps also prepared herself for the worst outcome in due course.

Shweta, who was now in her early forties, wore smart glasses over fair skin, smartly dressed as good as for a dentist. She carried smooth, silky hair, a broad forehead, steady eyes, and a slightly stout character. She was shorter than Shalini but taller than her mother. Her movements and body language spelt her success as a successful dentist in a metro city like Delhi. After completing her BDS, she also specialised in pediatric dentistry. Shweta was one of the most noted dentists in her space and boasted a long list of tiny clients of highly respected parents in Delhi.

After settling her mother, Shweta acknowledged with a slight nod of her head to Shalini and rushed to see her father. Devayani accompanied her in. She was distraught to see her father haplessly lie on one side of the bed, looking with eyes deep seated in the sockets, with a tinge of despair. She sat beside him and held his hand in hers. It was an old wrinkled hand, trying to search for the touch and accept its warmth. Yeshwant had shed far too many kilos during his short stay at the hospital, and it would have taken him, at least five times the period to gain some lost weight back.

Shweta spoke in a soft voice to Yeshwant." Baba, I have come. I will be around now for the next few days and will look after you to see you walking and chatting with me." Yeshwant only blinked his eyes. His acknowledgement was a visual evidence of resignation to fate. That despair in his sheepish but helplessly hesitant smile did not miss any of the eyes in the room, including Shalini's, who by then was occupied in the door frame of the room.

Shweta cleaned the dried saliva around Yeshwant's lips with a wet wipe tissue lying on the side table and sat beside her father for some more time, even as Devayani and Shalini left the room in some time.

She began to browse through the medical files, the discharge summary, and the overall reports of her father to study and infer medically what he was staring at.

What Shalini deduced with her experience and analysis of the situation by going through it, Shweta established by studying it pathologically.

Siya had some cosy moments with her grandma and she dragged her feet into the room where her grandfather was ailing. She was accompanied by Arjun to make her feel comfortable.

Arjun performed all the humble acts of a son-in-law to perfection and subtly impressed upon the house that another man had arrived to help them ease out of this situational mess. He was a senior corporate banker, and though he was better at numbers than emotions, he read the situation well and extended his warmth to the family in need.

The paramedic, Gopal, who was one more member in the house, stepped in to perform some cleaning duties for his patient and all the guests in the room were asked to leave.

As Shweta and Arjun were settling down in the role of the new torchbearers, Shalini's mind began to wander and plan for her return. She felt obliged that she should stay for a day more to overlap with Shweta's, as even she was meeting her younger sibling after many months, perhaps years. The joy of reuniting with her sister was confounded by the dreadful event, and both could not even express the joy of meeting each other after a hiatus.

She wished she had more time with Shweta, some fun time.

Within a day, Shalini downloaded all the medicinal routine to Shweta and Devayani, though Gopal was well in charge and doing his job, to the satisfaction of all the house occupants.

Shalini spent some good time with her niece coming of age. She was academically bright and expected to fare well in her board exams. As she was engaged in an absorbing discussion with her niece, she remembered Shaunak and the worries and concerns of his, took over her mind, which was just being emptied from Yeshwant's worry, albeit partially.

She fretted with the old problems at hand, as if to wake them up from a short slumber. Shaunak, Murugan, and all the other concerns which kept her nervously occupied resprouted, and she took the early morning flight the next day back to Bengaluru to confront them afresh.

The flight took off on time and landed on time. 'Such flights which take you back to your problems, never get delayed,' she wondered, as if destiny wanted her to start facing challenges she had pocketed, again, as quickly as possible. She first chose to head home and join the office chaos post lunch.

Santosh

As Santosh chatted with Arjun over the phone and got a recent 'male version' of the situation, he realised that there was a challenge to be overcome and the outcome did not look easy. Not easy on the eyes, nor easy on the mind, and perhaps not easy on the pockets too. However, the affluent daughters of Yeshwant would have taken care of the last one easily, and Yeshwant himself would have been well placed to bear the pinch, after those many years of service and savings, even after the marriages of the daughters.

He had a brief thought journey into the health of his parents and had made a short visit to them as he had flown down, one of the weekends, to see Yeswant get discharged from the hospital. As Yeshwant got settled in his house, Santosh sped to be with his parents.

Madhusudan and Yashoda were happy to see their son. Both the septuagenarians were elated to see their son, though an unpleasant happening had brought him to town.

Even during a brief stay at home, Yashoda made some delicacies which would tickle the taste buds of her son, who had a special longing for food, and specially that made by his mother.

Madhusudan took that chance to discuss the inheritance with his son, and though Santosh wanted to avoid that topic, Madhu insisted upon him to lend him ears. A conservative investor as he was, Madhu had more faith in the conventional modes of savings- bank deposits. Being a banker himself made it easier for him to ride that route.

Santosh and Shalini had enough accumulated wealth to take care of themselves and their son. Being the only son, all his father's wealth would also have accrued to Santosh, including the house in Khar, worth millions. He was not particularly interested in the quantum but Madhu wanted to keep his son informed about his financial matters. Yeshwant's sudden collapse made him nervous, and he thought of sharing his intricacies with his son before he too became incommunicado.

The human mind assumes the speed of light when it comes to running. And when it comes to the greying of hair, many untoward thoughts queue up and fight to claim the podium and render one restless. Madhu was nervous with the degeneration of Yeshwant and had a vicarious uneasiness with the thought that he could be next in line.

As he started brooding over it, he felt that he should empty his financial frame to his son and feel relieved of having downloaded all of it, especially when Santosh was physically there, and he himself was fit to discuss.

Madhu led a very simple life, as most of the middle-class or just higher-middle-class Indian family men would. That simple life, not a very demanding wife and an only son, who was self-made, filled his coffers well. He was content with this wealth accumulation and happy that he could leave it behind for Santosh to take care of his mother, should he win the exit race with his wife.

Santosh heard him patiently, although reluctantly. He had already imagined the plight of health any of his parents would undergo, should anyone be defeated by their ageing body. The thought had made him edgy. No matter how old one grows, one remains the child of the parents, and no matter how old the parents grow, they remain the support and guide of the child. Santosh was in his fifties, but still the child of his parents, the only child.

He had seen Shalini's quandary from the corners of his mind when Yeshwant took ill and imagined his condition when any of his parents took to the hospital bed. As emotional and timid, he could grow more at the trigger of the event. Santosh had gone into his own shell and brewed diffidence. Only the realisation that he needed to head to Bengaluru and take charge of his work and home brought him to peace.

Escapism often works well when it comes to confronting anxious matters.

As was the case with Shaunak and all beings, Santosh was also governed by the play of the gunas. In the dilapidated state of mind, the *Tamas* guna took charge, overpowering the other two gunas that rested within him and made him spiral down the path of timidity. Only when he would gather himself and refocus on his growth, family and goals, the *Rajas* guna gained prominence and pulled him temporarily out of the negative spiral and hesitancy.

This cyclical up and down continued with Santosh, as with many of us, who are stirred through this journey of emotions and uncertainty.

Santosh was not only crammed in the play of his gunas, but between the feeling of care and apathy for his ailing parents. He criticised himself for not being able to take adequate care of his parents, being away from them and at the same time, felt hassled with the thought that he was the only one who would have to run around and carry on his shoulders, the onus of managing them.

What Santosh observed was that Yashoda had begun to forget a few things as he had a brief connection with her physically after a while. Not that it won serious proportions, but Santosh was fretted with the thought that it could be the beginning of the old age mental illnesses like Dementia.

He was fresh from the site where another close elderly man was encompassed by the clutches of his brain breakdown, his state of mind made him quickly believe that his mother was in store for a mental endeavour too. The fickleness of his mind and his natural tendency to linger over quickly, made him visit that lane of uneasiness and portended too far in his mind. Only that his trip was a short one, made him sidetrack the thought over other prominent issues.

Santosh was back and got back to his routine after a small, flying visit to Mumbai. Shalini's absence kept their home incomplete and blue. The only silver lining to her absence was the improved communication between the son and his father. Her prolonged absence made Shaunak engage with his father more than ever, and the easygoing but gradually maturing adolescent began to connect more with his father. Not because of the right reason, but Santosh grabbed it with both hands, which further improved his collaboration with Shaunak.

In all those many days when Shalini was in Mumbai, Shaunak ensured he spent most of his time at home rather than staying away with friends and Sayona.

Sayona also understood the gravity of the situation and gave him the space he deserved. Being in love with him and desperately seeking reciprocation, she exhibited exceptional maturity to let Shaunak focus on his family. As she began to faintly collect Shaunak's reciprocation, she did not want him to be alienated from her even with the silliest of reasons. All above, she did not miss to call him twice a day, during the day and at night, to enquire the status of his grandfather, but more to hear his voice and feel associated by just talking to him. She missed his presence even when he was around her in college and compensated by letting him know she cared for him, over those daily calls.

Very often, she used to exclaim to herself that in the family of S'es, Shalini, Santosh and Shaunak, another S, 'Sayona' would fit well. She used to feel elated with that funny thought.

Santosh was glad to have Shalini back. He was desperately waiting to see her back. He was worried for her. Though he had a brief sight of her during his visit to Mumbai, it was only now that he would confront her in solitude, especially after that Sunday fight organised by Murugan, after which many things unfolded dramatically.

Afterall, he was a perfect family man. Shalini and Shaunak were his life. Yashoda and Madhu occupied a special part of his heart, and so did Yeshwant and Devayani.

A family-oriented man draws strength from seeing their loved ones thrive. He always took time for his family, no matter how stressed or busy he was, and they tended to follow family values.

Being family-oriented means more than just loving your family—it's living for your family. During each assessment, Santosh always passed with flying colours. That he made a quick dash to Mumbai, all to show his care for Yeshwant, make his old parents happy with his sight and render support to his wife in her lonely battle, were all testimonials of that.

Days passed, Shweta returned to Delhi, Devayani got used to looking after the immobile Yeshwant with the help of Gopal and his deteriorated health condition, refusing to improve, became an accepted, routine condition of life for all the cast involved.

Shalini

Shalini was home, but she was not comfortable staying there. She had a fleeting face-off with Shaunak and Santosh before they both stepped out for their work. She wanted to stay home and relax, but she could not. What an irony! She was dying to be back home, to be free from the clutches of the added responsibility she was imposed upon, around her father's health, desperate for Shweta to share her load and relieve her, and spare some time reposing by unwinding all she had gone through in the last two-three weeks. That time at home, where she was the most eligible denizen, was ideal to undergo that transformation and cleansing. She was perturbed to find out that she got those key moments to recharge and hoe out the unpleasant vibes, but could not capitalise on them. She was helplessly watching the clock tick off, and approaching lunch time, and more specifically, the time for her to leave for her office.

She had made sure earlier in the day that she had a chat with Shweta and Devayani and diligently carried out her earnest duties towards her maternal family.

But she was totally restless in the house, and was carrying some eerie feelings within. She wasn't sure what the feelings meant. An Omen?

She had chatted with her mother, and that chat did not throw out any negative connotations. The other area which could have been smelling danger was her office. She uncannily was portending something ominous to take place there.

"Can't destiny take pity on me? I am back from a saddening return, bringing my father from a life-threatening situation to no better than a struggling life, dependent and having a terminal outcome." She pitied herself.

She began to think aloud, "Don't I deserve even some compassion from the destiny to at least spare me from some anxious moments now at the office, especially when I have gone through plenty already?

"Or I am trying to read too much into my uneasiness?" She tried to console herself.

The fact that she had quite spooky feelings was tending to bring her to some heralds that something else, something unkinder was in store.

A woman is sometimes blessed with a sixth sense, and she can catch the impending vibes far more easily, be it a lewd eyesight of some lecherous man, someone trying to be too jealous with her or something threatening looming large. Shalini innocently belonged to that category.

She did not even remember what she had for lunch, which Yogini had cooked for the family earlier in the morning. She, however, recollected the short but compassionate dialogue she had with Yogini and her extending warm regards and consolation to her. Yogini had seriously felt for her mistress, who was always kind to her. Yogini respected Shalini for all she had achieved, and was further in her awe, for her responsibility towards her parents. She knew the worry Shalini carried for her son, and she watched her changing life from close corners.

Shalini completed her lunch, and as if being pulled to, she dashed towards her office. Being a quieter period of the day, she had less difficulty navigating through the traffic of the city, and she entered the office premises with a heavily pounding chest.

As her colleagues caught her sight, they approached her in numbers to check her whereabouts, her father's condition and extended to her their moral support, in words and by being around. With colleagues and office friends around, she felt well supported and a heavy load was off her back. It was after a long gap that she felt relieved, considered, and accommodated.

Shalini, her habit and tendency to remain connected and updated, kept her emails and responses to emails upto date, and when she looked at them afresh, from her office seat, she did not feel out of touch.

By the time it clocked four, and the cubicles rose for a tea break, Shalini was summoned by Murugan. She hurriedly moved to his cabin and her heart began to pound again, as it had when she had entered the office premises.

Shalini entered Murugan's cabin with her heart in her mouth. She was fearing that she would be moved out of the project, and her absence from the office might have allowed several aspirants to lobby against her, squeeze in entry and establish soft equations to win their claims.

Murugan, with his signature poker face, wasted no time and relayed to Shalini that she would be issued a 'pink slip' and would need to serve two months of notice before her services would come to an end. She was being served with a garden leave clause where; after serving her resignation notice (factually being terminated), she would have required to stay away from work during the notice period while remaining on the company's payroll. She would have continued to receive her salary and benefits. but not harm the employer's interests during this period in any way.

Shalini was aware of such a drive to clean up the middle management in their company recently, and their project status did not keep her comfortable ever since. That Monday presentation, which ate up her entire Sunday, was a premonition of sorts to that. But the meeting with their vice president some fortnight back did not send her such immediate signals, and she believed that she had a bit more time. Murugan did not even give her the hint when she was away, and waited for her return to apprise her of the hostile outcome, in person. He was a seasoned campaigner.

Shalini was speechless. Her vibes that had turned negative were some indicators of this consequence. At first, she got stung by the bug of rejection. She felt unwanted, rejected, and unworthy of herself. With the travails she had for the last few years, her tussles with Murugan, and that which led to her skirmishes with Santosh, her bodily wearing out, all had taken toll on her. She had wanted to quit so many times, at each unbecoming instance, but never crossed over. She wondered why she did not choose to decide to quit and continued in the rut.

She wanted to leave gracefully and on her own choice. But at that moment, she regretted that she failed to make the decision by herself. And that day, she was served a notice to count her numbered days for her employer.

With the first feeling of self-criticism that arose almost instantaneously, she pondered deep within and realised the embarrassment, humiliation, and self-pity she might then have needed to suffer. So many thoughts gathered in her mind, and each thought dislodged other in no time.

She looked into Murugan's eyes. The ruthless face that he always wore, Murugan had no compassion for her, nor any remorse that he was made to do the dirty job. He was a veteran and had umpteen such previous instances where he had played the villain or the bad cop.

The Human Resources department also felt it was easier to get it done through him than to get bad-named in the eyes of the victims.

"Shalini, the board is critically evaluating areas of bringing the costs down. A large chunk of middle management is shelved off, and soon, senior management will also fall in line. You know I am managing 3 projects right now and had to pick up a few who would ease off the burden on costs. You are one of them," Murugan served his measured explanation to her.

"Who else?" Shalini enquired out of curiosity and for self-consolation. Getting to know a few more would not have made her suffering less, but being a part of a larger whole would have perhaps made her agony less painful.

The seasoned pickle, as he was, Murugan retorted," You will know soon. Such things do not remain hidden for too long."

He knew exactly how to handle such situations. He then started to sugarcoat the episode by giving her suggestions based on his experience.

Murugan had always come across as a task master. He never allowed anyone to enter into his space, and neither did he enter others'. He had employed all the tools and measures to reach that position of a senior director and trampled all the obstacles that came in his path of progress, not all by choice, but some by necessity too.

A diligent manager, with extremely astute communication and planning skills, he rose through the ranks and earned his place as a tower of dependability in the company. He had managed several projects, good and dirty. Not that he did not make mistakes, but his exemplary work and management skills overrode those slip-ups, and he rode his own path of progress.

Murugan knew that all was not well in the company of late, and even his days were numbered. Only that picking up Shalini and a few like her would keep his position in the line safer for some time at least then.

In his late fifties, Murugan's only son was married and settled in the US. His wife was a fine arts protagonist and had her world of art and creations well covered. He had achieved as much as he might have wanted. He did not carry the ambition of becoming the CEO, and his own achievements and family stability never kept him confused. He thus became a ruthless achiever in his tenure and seemed to hold little empathy towards people.

He had left only a few years before he would officially retire if all went well. But signs of all being well were far from the truth. The company was sinking under the fiercely competitive environment. Downsizing, though they were terming it as right sizing, was an omnipresent phenomenon across the industry. His company wasn't any different.

Murugan was a sorted beast. He never took things too deeply into his heart and kept it simple and stupid. He was result-driven to the core, and that made him seemingly callous and curt.

He never took matters of office at home, despite being vigorously demanding. He had an uncanny knack of leaving office matters over there before reaching home. Though he needed to work later at home, attend calls, and spend Sundays, he kept all emotional matters at bay and approached all the same with composure as part of his role. His wife was well versed with this and never raised a complaint. She was proud of her husband's intelligence and achievements and never crossed his path.

"All this quick, Murugan?" Shalini pleaded.

"Shalini, this was coming. I knew this was coming. But I had less scope to change it. You have been an asset to me, and I always relied on your competence, your problem-solving attitude, and your amicable ways to manage our team. Your progress has been remarkable, and you are one of the most softspoken, endearing colleagues I have worked with. The compulsions of the job never let me extend these pleasantries with you, or they were perhaps my nature's limitations, which curbed me from expressing it upfront with you anytime in the past," Murugan disclosed.

"The highlight and perhaps the low point of my way of working is my inability to express my emotions. I always assess individuals, comprehend how much I can push them to the wall, but I never had the vocabulary to praise them openly for their work and accomplishments, support, and contribution. You have a future ahead of you and at least a decade of work life. I am sure you will find some very decent path forward. I wish I could have shared my feelings about you with you a little earlier. But even though I may be reaching sixty, I too am learning," Murugan admitted.

"I understand," Shalini pretended to have aligned with Murugan.

Shalini was in a distraught mood. She was shattered by the sudden turn of events. When she was in Mumbai, she was restless and exasperated to be back in Bengaluru to take up the reins and break free from the depressing air at her home. She rose in the morning and, leaving all the lethargy, fatigue, and physical toll of the last many days behind her, she rushed to reach the office, only to be served a harsh sentence. She was bemused by the unfavourable fortune she was wearing for the last many months.

She was finding a way to reconcile with this concussion. She pitied herself with the sequence of misfortune, and in this swamp of self-pity, she was taken aback by that suddenly confronted unknown facet of Murugan.

She was trying to assess whether she found the soft and sensitive part of Murugan, or it was a routine, deceptive red herring disclosure by him. She had no choice but to believe through the former. She, even in that broken mood, felt proud of herself to be conscious of prudence.

She spent some more time with Murugan chatting about many matters, which were getting increasingly irrelevant to her, and soon she rose from her chair, shook hands with him, and turned away to the exit.

It was nearing five in the evening, and Shalini felt no reason to keep herself working in the office, which had numbered her days, only some minutes back. She tried to keep her face as the same as it was before she met Murugan, and any displeasure on her face would only be attributed to the medical condition of her father, and nothing else, which she carried as she walked into the office, at least for her office colleagues.

Shalini wrapped her belongings from her working table, shut her laptop down, grabbed her purse and headed for her home. Murugan was observing her movements from the plain part of his taped glass cabin walls, with his signature indifferent face.

She was bothering Santosh enough with so many daily ills and was feeling embarrassed to add one more unpleasantry to him, later in the day. She thought of calling him right then and sharing the devastating news, but gathered courage and patience to stay put till evening when she would meet him in person.

She was supposed to hand over her laptop and all office belongings the next day. She remembered that as she slid the laptop into her backpack, thinking aloud in her mind that it was the last time she did that act.

She operated the biometric to exit the office door, and as she was pulling the door in; to walk out, she wondered how many more times she would have to scan her finger on the biometric scanner. She waited for the lift to take her from the eleventh floor and greeted a few officemates while waiting.

The lift arrived and took her to the ground. It was the fastest travel to the ground floor she had ever experienced, after working for years in those premises.

"How quickly I have reached the bottom!" She exclaimed in resignation.

She waited for the cab to take her home, and as she waited for the cab, she felt like not going home. "But if not home, where?" she mercifully asked herself.

Too many cheerless thoughts got strewn on her mind's horizon. She felt she was being scooped hollow from within. She even started to hate herself. Shalini had only recently praised herself when she could try to find out the meaning behind Murugan's words despite being in a hysterical state. And now, she was feeling worthless and had a very low self-esteem. She felt like yelling out loud, and express her frustration over all that she had no control over, but made her sweat her heart out.

In the negative spiral of mental journey, she ran through the ups and downs of her career and revisited her achievements and testimonials. Even in that blue state of mind, she felt elated with the memory of some of her attainments and feats. She was glad that when he flashbacked on her past, she could pick a few things to root for.

Early evening, it was less congested. As it turned out, she was brought home by the cabbie very quickly. Though she was engrossed in her scheme of thoughts, she found herself at to the home premises very quickly. She chuckled with the thought that all worldly matters had colluded to bring her back home as quickly as possible. Even the dreadful traffic lent her its mercy, she felt.

She climbed up through the elevator to their well-crafted home and unlatched the door to see the familiar furnishings, interiors, and lighting. Was the house looking brighter?' she thought. She felt that she had more time at hand and could stare deep into the home after a long time. She began to acknowledge the fact that she was going to have more time now to look deep into this trivia.

She brewed herself a coffee, granting herself that luxury. As she sipped her coffee, she placed herself back on the thought train and began reminiscing about the journey she had thus far. From her first job, and to that day, she scrutinised each milestone she reached and began to self-assess only to soothe herself and regain her confidence. As she plunged into the game of rumination, it was quite dark in the evening. She had lost track of the daylight and twilight too as she kept digging in.

Santosh unlatched the door to find Shalini staring through the balcony, into the darkening sky in an unilluminated room. As he saw her from behind, sitting all by herself, he sensed she was in a deep indigo mood, and Yeshwant could be the reason for that. He felt for his wife.

He switched on the room lights, and that made Shalini turn around. She was relieved to see Santosh, and she had tears rolling down her cheeks as she caught his sight.

Santosh feared for Yeshwant and approached Shalini to get more vibes from her.

"Santosh, I have been served a pink slip and expected to be free in two months from tomorrow. All the efforts I have been putting in have yielded no results. I am getting thrashed from all corners. I am feeling disgusted," she pleaded with him.

Santosh was moved. He hadn't expected this in all his basket of conjectures when he had seen Shalini in the dark, staring at the sky. He kept his office bag aside, got his shoes off and stepped towards Shalini. She wanted him to come close to her and hug her with warmth.

Santosh went closer to her, and she almost fell into his arms. She gave out a subdued whimper, and he caressed her forehead. She wanted that touch of temperateness. A few moments passed without a word being uttered. Shalini let her emotions flow. All those emotions synthesised and found their way out in the form of subdued tears.

After a few seconds, Shalini gathered herself. She got up, wiped her nose, wiped her eyes and looked into Santosh's eyes with vulnerability.

Santosh got disturbed by that sight. He might have fought with her, wanted to have been a shade more successful than her and a wheeler-dealer in some sense when it came to comparing the two. But he would have never wanted her to get scoured and wounded like this.

"You have no reason to feel sorry or worry, Shalu," Santosh reassured her.

"I know what you are, what you have done thus far, and what you have gone through. You need to hold your head high, and I will always be proud of you."

Shalini felt as if ice cubes were poured over her frenzied body, and she gulped a sigh of relief.

"You weren't working for money, but pride and now you should step back and find new areas to search for your pride. I stand by you in your search and new journey," Santosh added.

Shalini was so relieved to have an understanding and caring husband.

Shaunak joined the pair in good time, and the three of them had a family dinner together after many weeks.

As she was about to retire for the day, Arjun called Shalini. She felt that the sequence of bad news was just not over. She shakingly took his call.

Arjun elucidated at the start that he had called for an altogether different reason. That calmed her nerves and kept the conversation going with ease.

Arjun had his friend Akshay, who was working in Shalini's office, albeit in a junior role. Akshay was in a completely different vertical, but Arjun's childhood buddy. Shalini knew Akshay through Arjun's reference, and she only interacted with him occasionally, in the lobby, lift, or the canteen as she bumped into him.

Arjun first enquired how Shalini was, how Santosh was doing that evening and the whereabouts of Shaunak, and exchanged pleasantries. They also chatted about Yeshwant, and his fragile state which was reaching a new normal to all.

He added further, "Shalini, I learn from Akshay that your company is undergoing a major overhaul and many employees, mid-senior and senior, are asked to go. Please keep a track of and monitor these developments closely. I gathered from you that your project is sailing in a rough sea, and I thought of alarming you."

Shalini thanked Arjun as if to pretend she was not aware of the insider developments. She was trying to decipher whether her news was out in the company, and if Akshay dialled it to Arjun or that Arjun was genuinely concerned about her. Such news isn't guarded as a secret in offices, and the grapevine amplifies it loudly and pompously. Many names get discussed who are not even in the frame of things. Her unfortunately was, and she believed that she might have already become a name under discussion and murmurs.

She hung up by enquiring about her younger sister and niece. She did not want to speak with Shweta in that frame of mind and mood.

As they all hit the bed, Shalini rested her head on Santosh's chest and felt peaceful. Neither of them uttered a word, but their silence was reassuring and intimate. Shailini could not recollect how long she was pondering over the events of the day, but at some hour into the midnight she was in deep sleep, a sleep which she needed most.

The next day was like any other day, or rather, should have been. Yogini came to cook for the family, and she got into the job as a routine. She was surprised to find Shalini not in a hurry and concluded that the physical toll which she might have undergone for the last many days would have slowed her speed.

As Yogini was kneading the dough, she relayed to Shalini with her head down," Didi, Govind has lost his job again. The contractor messed up big time, and all got blacklisted. Govind will need to find a new contractor, and it will take him some time. Till then, I will be the engine of the house, once again."

Yogini was expressing this with a wry smile. It wasn't the first time that Govind had lost his job, and Yogini had taken over the reins.

Shalini felt bad and sympathised with a fellow sufferer. She was, however, amused to see how Yogini could purchase a smile even then. Just last evening, she was shattered, felt intensely worthless and both a victim and an offender. In a flash, she had thought that all roads had ended and she would get her reputation built over the years sublimated in a hurry.

"Will you have to face a serious financial crisis immediately?" Shalini asked Yogini

"Didi, we are used to this. Govind has not had a steady path of income, and we have witnessed this far too often. I have anchored my ship so that we can withstand the rough weather each time. We have only little savings that can help us for a month or two," Yogini elaborated.

"Govind came home yesterday, heavily drunk, and physically ill-treated me as if his losing his job was my fault. He hurled abuses and cast a mouthful of bad language. The mohallah was up in the street, pushed him to leave home and they escorted me to safety. When he got sober this morning, he returned home as if nothing had happened.," Yogini pressed upon.

"He will get a new job in a few days, and then some day again lose it for his fault or his boss's. Till then, I will keep batting to keep the scoreboard ticking," she continued.

Shalini kept thinking about what she heard. She got some enlightenment from one of the most unexpected corners.

Yogini and her way of life instilled a very important learning in Shalini. The pair of Yogini and her husband, who had hand to mouth situation, had Govind out of work, and Yogini came across as a prepared, intrepid, prudent, but circumspect lady who kept her nerves and deluged optimism in her words.

She was supposed to get mad with her husband, who, on losing his job, had the respite to rely on her, but on the contrary, beat her, abused her, and spent more money on drinking. Money! which would have helped them buy a few more necessities than draining it in liquor.

Shalini was perplexed by Yogini's behaviour. She was very impressed with her maturity at her age. Yogini was in her mid-thirties. The way she calmly and sensibly collected herself and oriented to the change was commendable. She wasn't thinking too far.

Shalini envied Yogini for having displayed such calmness when she was a far more deserving candidate to express anger, frustration, and despair. Shalini had consoled Yogini many times in the past, when Yogini had agonized around her childlessness. She had felt elderly while counselling Yogini by giving her some tips on life. And here, it was Yogini's turn to return the favours.

But as if she was overjealous that Yogini, her house help, who was less educated, less experienced, and quite younger to have given her simple lessons of life, she pretended to herself that all given, Yogini was wrong to have suffered the physical abuse and should have stood against it.

On reaching that thought, Shalini felt back deservingly elderly, mature, experienced, and feminist and had something to be honoured despite undergoing the lesson.

Happiness is largely a choice. While it is impossible to control everything that happens to you, you can control your internal thought processes, the actions, and the reactions. Ultimately, being happy with what you have is a matter of focusing on the good things in your life, letting go of unrealistic burdens and expectations, and doing your best to make yourself feel good in the here and now.

Getting off the burden, the baggage is the secret of pleasure, if not happiness. When the monkey is off the back, the load vanishes like magic.

Shalini had been served a hostile scenario. She had enough wealth to see her through for the rest of her life. Besides, she had a husband who was earning exceedingly well. Even if he had stopped earning, the pair would have easily survived for the rest of their lives, without needing to alter their way of life too much. Financial stability was not even an area to be concerned about.

When she was asked to leave, Shalini was nervous as the bundle of expectations she carried had been distorted. The burden of carrying the image in the extended family, the society, and friends to be a successful, self-made woman who holds serious positions. The burden of carrying the imposed expectations on oneself. Those expectations and the self-pride of having been able to carry those easily all these years had kept her mindful. That was shattered more than anything else, and she had a more pronounced and conspicuous reaction.

As she dwelt deeper, she realised the frivolity of her state and her responses to the stimuli, since the previous day. She began to repose into equilibrium, but once again questioned, 'Why me?'

After another battle of nerves and dialogue with herself, she began to fall to the right side of broader thinking and decided to accept that change with grace, and investigate areas which she always wanted to explore, enjoy, and feel fulfilled.

Areas, she could not narrow down on till then! She made up her mind to enter newer frays and face life with a new perspective.

Change is what she had wanted many times in the last few months. But what change she never could imagine or decide. It was just that fortune, or misfortune, had impressed upon her the opportunity to embrace that change.

She got up and readied to go to the office to start the handover process. As she walked to her bedroom, she could sense the spring in her steps, even if it was three-quarters deliberate.

Shalini reached the office. The office was working as normal. People were moving around, some with their necks sunk deep into their computer screens, some on their phones, and so on. She entered the office around 11:30 AM. As she entered, a few necks turned around to trace her. This would have been natural for people to notice someone walk through the aisle, but Shalini thought that she was singled out and everyone was sparing themselves to watch her as if they wanted to see the victim of the management crackdown, live.

She walked straight into Murugan's cabin. She now needed no permission or appointment to seek his time anymore. As Murugan caught her sight, he signalled her to take her seat.

Murugan stared into her eyes and tried to catch her mood. Shalini, by now, had gathered much courage to give a stern look back into his eyes. Murugan fumbled with that unexpected response from her, and quickly winked his sight off her. Her firm eye contact told him much more than he might have thought she would have wanted to convey to him, after that almost one-way communication last evening in private.

As she was granted the garden leave, she wasn't expected to work anymore and handover the jobs at hand, the company-owned paraphernalia she carried with her and all documents, authorisations, and power of attorneys she possessed, back.

Murugan, a man of chosen words, did not extend his verbal communication with her again and wished her good luck for her future endeavours. Shalini thought she had decoded Murugan, but she perhaps hadn't.

Shalini pushed his glass cabin door and stepped out to confront the crowd, who by now had learnt about her exit.

She walked straight to her desk, and as she reached there, her team enclosed her working space. She quickly learnt that Pankaj, Yogesh, Saritha and Vishwanath were a few other casualties whom she knew. As she found herself on a list with a few others, she felt less embarrassed than before.

She could sink in her status, and gradually began to find the carriers of change for her. She did not think of updating her social media status yet.

A couple of weeks passed. Shalini was getting used to staying away from the office. Not required to dig through a mountain of emails, responding to the ones that mattered and managing all coworking and hierarchical relations, was such a welcome change for her. Was that what she wanted as the change? She still wasn't sure, but she began to enjoy that peace.

In Mumbai, Devayani had started to increasingly confide in Gopal. She got used to his support and began to rely on his services she paid for. She started to move out, to get the groceries, sort banking matters and even visit friends and relatives to be back before late afternoon. She had accepted Yeshwant's fate. In the initial days, she felt too burdened to move out, connect with the outside world and felt like she had to force herself to confine, as any overt and outward act would be seen with disconcert. She was consumed by this self-induced dichotomy, and as it happens, gradually quite so often, she resumed her life.

To the north of Mumbai in Delhi, Shweta and Arjun had reorganised themselves and worn their routines. They had planned to have an overseas vacation once Siya had completed her board exams, but with Yeshwant, steady but ill, they had dissuaded themselves of such a plan and had hung it over, for some other day.

The Upadhyayas too got engulfed in their routines, gradually, and by habit. Their Bengaluru friend circle rejuvenated once again, and life began to travel as if it had a brief stopover and the journey began for the destination, the destination which none was completely clear of.

After the initial few days, Shalini now had got newly squeezed between the change she aspired for and the catalyst of that change, her dismissal from the job. Her mind was at work again.

Shalini would have regular update calls from Devayani and had occasional telephonic conversations with Yashoda and Madhu. It had been a month since Yeshwant was brought back home, but he showed little progress. The assured Mumbai routines made her satisfied, though it was superficial and artificially implied.

During this period, Shalini began to look for ideas, options, and avenues to engage herself once again. She spent time watching reels, videos and social media content on nature, hiking, fitness, and nutrition.

She began to develop a liking for it and started to get into more of that.

Santosh

As he came back from Mumbai, he wanted to share his worries about his mother with Shalini. Such things could not have been talked over the phone. He waited patiently for her to be back, to open her his apprehension.

She came within a few days of his wait, and Santosh decided to share his concerns with her that evening. But the evening he confronted her was a picture not even imagined in the frame.

He was himself aspirational but never let Shalini sacrifice for him. That they both stayed in Bengaluru, the capital of the IT Industry in India, which always secured them with ample opportunities, even if any one opportunity went begging. But as they grew in stature and position, the opportunities began to shrink. Despite this, both Santosh and Shalini relied on their experience, expertise, and capability to keep making inroads.

But as he found Shalini devastated with her ouster, he had to extend all his warmth to her to get her out of the trauma.

He and Shalini had talked through the future several times in the past. Over a late morning coffee on one lazy Saturday when Shaunak had remained adhered to his bed, the couple had some intimate moments of chat which outlined and schemed out their further path. They confided in each other and always stayed assured with the financial position they had. They had very secure finances, no major liabilities except the advances that might have been required for their son's future. But even that was well covered. So, any of them having a rough time and needing to stop working would never have affected them financially. They thought they were also prepared for that casualty if it arose.

As destiny would have it, it was Shalini's term to be chosen first. The assuring discussions she had with Santosh in the past about stability and abundance did not come to her rescue. When they both were collected and stable, they had discussed this possibility and had vowed to gulp it without too much displacement of the mind. But when it actually dawned, she was torn apart by her removal.

The intellect is a sorted-out sense. It chooses and readies to walk around the rational lane, and prepares to embrace the consequences after a well thought-over and mindful series of predispositions. But when it comes to undergoing the unforeseen, the mind takes full control of the intellect, makes it dance to its tune, and gifts it with doubts, fears, and shams. The intellect, so very powerful and capable, slowly becomes the slave of the mind.

Santosh had tacitly realised that the lifestyle they sported, the societal pride they carried, made it unknowingly mandatory for them to boast their status, through their demeanour, their standard of living and overall appearance and presence. They no longer needed the money they earned to meet their needs, but needed to hold jobs with those packages to flaunt their worth and value. Those salary packages were never to be disclosed or discussed in public, were to be kept private but exhibited with the overall conduct in life.

The pride of wearing that well paid job!

The pride that displayed the capability and worthiness of being employed at that level.

Shalini winked. He felt a bit mystified by that response by Shailini, especially when they had numerous deliberations beforehand to be prepared to quit the job(s). He then honestly questioned himself, too. Even he agreed to himself that he would have floundered first, if it were to occur to him. Santosh was honest in his valuation. He also accepted the fallacy in their high-level, confounded, theoretical conversations, which got smashed at the first trigger itself. The intellect had surrendered to the mind in no time.

It took them time to ride over the change and come to terms. This period kept Santosh responsibly silent from sharing his concern about his mother.

During this period, Santosh tightened his grip on his job, as he now felt he was more responsible for holding on to his mettle than before. Not that he became a workaholic, but he grew his intensity, his orientation, and his position towards his role in office. This was a natural reaction to compensate for a small glitch the family had experienced on the career front.

It was around five months now that Yeshwant was ridden to his bed and showed only little signs of improvement. Devayani too got used to the palliative care Gopal provided him. She started to visit her friends, cousins, and peers over small, quick functions, simple celebrations, while Gopal took care in her absence. There were periods where Gopal used to absent himself for personal reasons and Devayani got his replacement seamlessly through the services bureau to keep the act going. Shalini was happy to see her mother taking the reins into her own hands. Though Yeshwant was now assured of his irrevocable phase of degeneration, Shalini thought Devayani would never be able to manage him independently. The mother had proven the mother of the young man wrong.

During the interim, both daughters had made quick visits to Mumbai to meet their ailing father and overworked mother. Even though Gopal was available, Devayani had to walk some extra miles for her husband. The Devayani of the hospital when Yeshwant was in his early days of ailment, and the Devayani then, some months later, were two different versions of the same person. Time delivers miracles. This was just a noticeable change.

In all the challenging, adverse world around the Upadhyayas, life had its own way ahead. Santosh got awarded a promotion in his job. He was promoted as a senior director, offered a good raise and a plethora of perks. He had an excellent appraisal and sat in the top 1% of the employees in his conglomerate company. He now reported to the Vice President and had dotted line reporting to the President of Indian Operations.

Santosh was thrilled with this turn of events. His firm grip on the job and his extra focus after Shalini's episode were rewarded handsomely. This had further tapered down any concerns or financial worries, including Shaunak's further education overseas, should they have decided it.

During that period when he found a lull in Shalini's mind, he had expressed his apprehension of the impending danger of dementia dangling over Yashoda's head. Shalini acknowledged the concern, but she either felt it was too premature to vex over or that, since she had borne all the onus when it was her father, she expected Santosh to bear all the cargo, and she would ably support him as needed. She was not ready to take on more mental challenge, at least for the time being.

Like Shalini, Santosh too had made some interim visits to his home, sometimes together with Shalini, met his ailing parents and reassessed his impression about Yashoda's health.

Old age is a Pandora's box and once opened, one is confronted with several consequences, many of which are undesirable and unexpected.

Santosh kept his impressions to himself with occasional sharing with Shalini, but did not go so far as to investigate further with medical assistance. Afterall, Yashoda had shown no great signs of deterioration yet, and even if she did, there was very little medical intervention to cure it, if it were Dementia. It could at best be slowed from faster disintegration. Santosh was aware of this and decided to spend his energy on other matters, as he believed it was only his presentiment.

The Bengaluru couple had begun to hang out with their friends at weekends and purchase some lighter moments in life. After a prolonged trough, the sinusoidal wave of life was reaching the crest.

All their friends in the circle were successful, achieving class, who were coeval to the financial and family status as theirs. They got along well, and many of their friends had kids who were almost of the same age as Shaunak's. The kids also got along well, as their parents did.

Time delivers, even this time it did, delivering some stability, solace, and recharge to the situation, which was deemed as a crisis, menace, and test of patience, only a few months back.

Shalini was relieved from her services, got her gratuity, provident fund and other severance benefits, and thus added handsomely to her bank balance and coffers.

The care and concern about Yeshwant and Yashoda too had gone into the second tier; as dull it might have been, it had routined over. Life had started to reorient and align to the new frontiers, once again.

Things started to fall in line. Shaunak was also on the last lap of his graduation and would have soon emerged as a bachelor in commerce. All started to fall in the picture-perfect frame, at least for the time being, for Santosh. He was more than content with what he had in store.

As happiness would also prick and pain, Santosh, who by now was rolling over leisurely, started to get itchy and edgy by thinking that he was missing something. For the last few years, he was so used to getting hurdled by several obstacles, he never reigned in perfect peace.

All in his lap now, but he still felt he had some empty coffers. He was bitten by this weird bug, but was unable to interpret what it was.

'Is it a problem of plenty? Or unease of abundance or shallowness of achievements realised?' Santosh thought to himself. He was enjoying this phase of life but as he used to calm himself down in solitude, he used to feel troubled and disturbed.

What an irony! A sedate childhood, which was decorated by hard academic achievements, a good marriage, no financial worries, an only son coming of age, no major responsibilities, and ills, but Santosh still felt that he was incomplete.

Like many middle-aged individuals like him, Santosh was confronted with the transition of identity and self-confidence.

Such a psychological crisis is brought about by events that highlight a person's growing age, inevitable mortality, and possible lack of accomplishments in life. Santosh started to undergo feelings of intense thoughts, remorse, and high levels of anxiety, and almost got up to make drastic changes to his current lifestyle, and even began to challenge the past decisions and events.

His cultural construct deepened this conflict within him. This encompassed the assigned value of money, conceptions of self, self-identity, class, other units of time, marriage, education, stereotypes, femininity and masculinity, and even the idea of 'social construct' itself. These are often not universal truths but relative landscapes that occupy the mind spaces. They arise from the collaborative consensus of the mind with no definitive answer.

Before Santosh could share this with Shalini, he expressed this to his buddy Partha, and Partha introduced him to Swami Yogeshwar.

Santosh was sandwiched between abundance and emptiness, fulfilment and inadequacy and satisfaction and lack of it. He had never leaned to the side of such support from spiritual gurus before. But Partha had insisted, and he asserted to himself that he would surely not lose anything or allow himself to lose. He thus decided to meet Yogeshwar, more due to Partha's weight, but also by an ulterior optimism that he might just earn some new way out.

Yogeshwar had a small ashram in Malleswaram and often drew large crowds, especially on weekends. It was a quiet Sunday, and Santosh arrived at the ashram, along with Partha. Partha was a regular attendee there, and many volunteers seemed to know him. He walked through the crowd as a seasoned visitor, and Santosh only followed Partha's path.

Partha brought him straight into the main pandal and got himself and Santosh a vantage seating position. Yogeshwar was about to arrive and deliver his Sunday dose of wisdom to his devotees. Yogeshwar was a much evolved and genuine sage who chose not to have a one-on-one face-off with his devotees but delivered the aspects of spiritual wisdom to a gathering of people to get awakened, comprehend the real purpose of existence and made them realise the chase behind illusions to achieve inner peace. He spoke exceedingly well, and his content was par excellence.

After around a quarter of an hour's wait, a fiery, majestic man, who could be in his mid-fifties, clad in a white robe, with well-trimmed, longish beard, longish, greyish hair, decently built and moderately tall, entered the pandal and took the centre stage. All the devotees who had assembled by then stood in his respect. He sent a gradient smile to all the attendees and signalled them to take seats.

Yogeshwar had decided to convey his thoughts on dualism and finding the true self on that day. He had aimed at withdrawing his audience from the illusory grip of material achievements, which deliver momentary pleasures. He first made each attendee realise that they were all there because each of them felt incomplete despite achieving well.

He continued. "Some of you might have been pressed upon by physical pains, mental agonies, rifts in relations, predicaments in jobs, dejected by failures, or just simply not happy. You are here to find a magic cure and restore normalcy. I wish I had one and handed it over to each one of you. And let us imagine I had, and I gave it to each one of you, and you got rid of the worries you brought here. But isn't this a temporary cure? The current set of worries and problems might disappear, but new ones will take their place, even without your knowledge, and you will continue to struggle, try your way, and when you feel you have no recourse, you will want to come back again for that magic cure. How long will you want to continue?"

Santosh was impressed by this first soliloquy by Yogeshwar. He had thought that Partha had brought him to a stereotypical guru who would feign powers to cure people's worries. But Yogeshwar came across as a wise, evolved individual who had sight on the deeper connotations of life.

Yogeshwar added, "We are beings that embody many emotions, taking the form of a human as born. They have become a part of our daily lives. Anger, greed, jealousy, pride, lust, and attachment are not just our curses; they take charge of our minds. As affirmed by the saints, we have been told several times 'Do not let the mind imagine unnecessary facets. Let the experiences of life take their own course.'"

"Yet we are still bound by the journey of thoughts, impressed by the emotions that spread like fire. Our entire emotional state and thought structure are entwined by them. Life is an endless, incessant game bound by these limitations. In this game, we naturally enjoy the pleasures of the moment, but with them come fear, anxiety, instability, a restless mind, frustration, boiling, and sorrow. Once we awaken from this illusion and the pain becomes unbearable, then a particular question arises: Who am I beyond this? Is this 'I' real or merely an illusion?"

"The struggle to seek knowledge begins here. It gives a hint that 'I' am merely a part, a part of a larger plan. The plan that is vast, cosmic. The unfulfilled wishes or *Vasana* bring prior karma to this earth in the form of a new life. 'We' and the actual role are not real; it is illusory, magical, and temporary. At a certain moment, the mind gets prepared to achieve the audacity to break free from this illusion's grasp. The doctrine of Triputi (A collection of three things that are related to each other, like the Knowable, Knower and knowledge) is the reason for the awareness of 'I'; it is an extension of the illusion itself. Therefore, the three qualities or the gunas (*Sattva*, *Rajas*, and *Tamas*) and the five elements – air, water, earth, sky and fire- arising from them are also manifestations of this illusion. The state known by the words - Sat-Chit-Ananda - being aware, is surprisingly the form of the illusion. In fact, once one reaches this state, it is beyond description in words."

"The illusion makes the mind waver in the form of thoughts and determines by enveloping the intellect. To have the 'awareness of existence' means to be. And if there is awareness, existence appears; else, how will that being express itself? Being in union with the Supreme Soul is the true essence. In this undisturbed, unexpressed form, how will the awareness of being or anything else even arise? The sense of 'I' will cease. Then how will existence be expressed? A being will only appear in relativity when there is duality. When everything becomes one, then there will be no one left to perceive or make a being appear distinctly separate. There, the illusion disappears effortlessly. Duality and non-duality are relative to each other so how will the sense of separateness be felt in non-duality?"

He dug deeper, "We have forgotten the original form of self, due to duality. The foam created by the waves on the seawater is no different from the sea itself. It is a part of the sea, it is the sea, yet it appears different. So am I. We have become certain that our current embodied form is the true essence of us as we appear separated from our true self. Being immersed in this illusion hinders the meeting with the ultimate reality. Identifying with that ultimate reality is our true form. Once this suspicion is rubbished and the oneness is achieved, the realisation of *Aham Brahmasmi* - All is the form of the universe, I am the universe - dawns."

Yogeshwar was speaking fluently and intently, and the attendees were spellbound. Some of them understood most of what he said, while some got a fleeting idea of the depth of his conveyance. It was Santosh's first exposure to this part of life, and he was impressed with Yogeshwar's philosophy, though he understood only some gist, albeit superficially.

He thought he found a lot of similarity between what he was going through and what Yogeshwar hinted at the symptoms of. He tried to pick the messages in parts and attempted to complete the jigsaw puzzle. He wasn't able to do it effortlessly, but underscored upon him to connect to this philosophy to help him find his way out.

Santosh, an academic intellectual, successful professional who had achieved all tangible highlights, was stuck in his own cobwebs of imagination and found light in the words of Yogeshwar. He and Partha approached Yogeshwar after the discourse and extended their gratitude to him. Partha introduced Santosh to Yogeshwar, and Santosh had a direct conversation with him. During the conversation, Santosh gathered that Yogeshwar himself was a rank holder CA, who had practised for over two and a half decades in several capacities before he plunged into this spiritual discovery. Santosh thanked him for his door opening for him and felt reassured that a journey on this path might put him on course.

In his state of bewilderedness, Santosh embraced a new pathway. He started to believe that his mind was an unbridled, untrained wild colt romping aimlessly through the confusion and doubts created by the self-imposed wilderness. He started to believe that he was easily vulnerable to external influences. He took it upon himself to steer his mind to the righteous path. He began to discover the path.

From a man who was a resolute achiever, caring family man, sensitive to his near ones, forthright and virtuous, but trapped in mundane possessions, fussed over failures and psyched by challenges; he had gotten exposed to the side of life, he never would have imagined and tried for.

Santosh, as he was driving back home, thought about how some Partha, whom he did not even meet daily, got shared his dilemma and how Partha took him to Yogeshwar, who opened the doors of spiritual mystic mystery to him to pacify his nerves and begin to seek knowledge, far beyond the ability to gain promotions, wealth, and material possessions.

Santosh was still not clear if he wanted to walk that path, but he was already bought over by that.

He thought of sharing that with Shalini as quickly as he could reach home. It was an early Sunday evening; the Bengaluru traffic behaved submissively and took him home soon.

Shalini

Shalini was getting used to life at home. She thought multiple times of joining the industry back through some other avenue, but every time she took a step forward, the need for 'change' clamoured in her head, and she turned her head away.

She slowly got used to the non-glamorous life at home. Life was less in charm, but more in peace, calmness, and time; time for the self. She wondered when she last had time, only for herself. It was always Santosh and then Shaunak, and then lately her parents. She had forgotten that she might also need to live for herself, cajole her interests and tastes. She had sporadic impulses to effect some change, but circumstances and the parasitic penchant for monotony sidestepped the intent each time.

An orchestrated event dissuaded her from that roguish routine and opened the boulevards to her to embrace some change.

During the first few days of being relieved from her office duties, she took time to give her tired body time to heal, repose and recuperate, although guiltily and hesitantly. Roving over social media handles which gave good insights on nature, hiking, and fitness caught her eyes.

Shaunak initially found it hard to see his working mother settle at home. He took pride in seeing his mother preen and resolute when she left for office, driving like a confident new generation woman. That she handled work on an international landscape made him extol her achievements. He never said a word to her, but silently admired her status. With her homecoming, he was a bit disappointed at the start.

Shalini noticed this disappointment in his eyes and his demeanour, but discarded that thoughtfully as a passing whim, without going to explain her side to her growing son. She became more assertive in finding space for herself and started to sink deeper into the areas she began to carve an interest in. This was a new path journey for her, but her ability to work through tougher situations had invoked an obstinate intent in her. She was now on a mission.

Shalini had joined groups which carried fitness freaks, within weeks of her homestay. From aerobics to jogging to cycling, she came across a new world of people who were passionately dedicated to physical fitness and maintaining a healthy lifestyle.

She began her trysts with early morning jogs and a fitness regimen. In came, quick-dry track suits, lightweight jogging shoes of the highest standards, wrist bands, and all the energy was aimed at reducing calories, flab and toning the body down. She was happy at her persistent initiative, which outlived two weeks and thus held it as her way of life going forward.

After a month of rigorous work and control over diet, Shalini was able to shed a few kilos. Women on the cusp of menopause develop a tendency to gain weight, and increased weight tends to enhance complications. The relationship between obesity and menopause is complex, influenced by a combination of hormonal fluctuations, lifestyle factors, and changes in metabolism.

Shalini was battling with menopausal challenges at her age, but getting her weight shed, was certainly going to have a positive impact on her. Also, feeling lighter made her feel more contented, and all these in combination were working well on her body, and its changes.

Over the last few years, Shalini and Santosh rarely came close. On the night of her last encounter with Murugan, she had taken Santosh's chest as a salvage place. It had been so many months; both had come physically close, more for an emotional shelter. However, on most of the nights, they stayed away. Even when they got up, the pillows were at some distance from each other. At their age, they expected more emotional support from each other than for physical needs. However, Santosh did not miss Shalini coming in her shape. He felt pleasant within.

Shalini had settled down in the fitness-oriented life of hers. Life was getting interesting and refreshing again, and she got the dreadful news that Yeshwant had finally succumbed to his prolonged illness. It was Mohan again to relay that dreadful news to her.

'Mohan again!' She had the first thought when she saw her phone ring. And this time Mohan went a few steps forward to convey to her the most unbecoming news. The Bengaluru family, as well as the family from Delhi, reached Mumbai in no time.

Yeshwant had wished that his mortal remains be donated for medical studies, and his daughters, along with their mother, obeyed his wish. The corpse of Yeshwant was duly handed over to Sir JJ Medical College after completing all due formalities. The small Purohit family was reduced by one. All grieved but recovered from the pain, the preparation of which had actually begun from the day Yeshwant was taken to the hospital.

During the same period, Yashaoda's forgetfulness also augmented but the doctor stopped short of diagnosing it as Dementia. Santosh and Shalini were relieved, but Madhu had a bigger role carved out.

Shalini, while in Mumbai, started to believe that she was once again shackled as 'daughter' and 'daughter-in-law' and whatever she had initiated as a fresh and new chapter of life could be nipped in the bud.

Shweta was always perceived as a younger sister who only cared for herself first. Shalini was the one who sacrificed more among the two. She was the one who took upon herself that additional responsibility. Both Shalini and Shweta stayed with their mother for some days. Shalini had no immediate compulsions to head back, but wanted to head back and embrace her newfound path. On the other hand, Shweta had kept her patients in the lurch. Tooth ailments are not emergencies, but cannot be delayed for long. Shalini was getting ready to carry her mother with her as her renewed responsibility next. To her surprise, Shweta insisted that Devayani join her at their home in Delhi. Siya, by then has enrolled in a famous junior college, *Corinthians*, and began to pursue her education in science. She was seen to be toeing her mother's feet in pursuing medical education.

Shweta had understood the delicate phase her elder sister was going through and advocated her new initiative. Shalini was mightily relieved as Devayani was taken along by Shweta to Delhi, at least for the time being. For the first time, Shalini felt she had prejudged Shweta, who deserved more admiration from her.

Shalini returned to Bengaluru and reconnected with her new way of 'fit life'. She joined her jogging sessions and rigorous training. She was slowly getting ready to participate in marathon runs. Her daily grind to get fit for the upcoming marathon then began with a resolute intent. It was backed by an adequate protein intake. Shalini had begun to live a totally different life from the one she lived till six months ago.

At her jogging sessions, she befriended new friends, most of them her age, who were drawn to this fitness regime, due to several reasons. She was pleased to find a few of them had reasons which matched hers.

Two months from then, she was on the running field, eagerly waiting to run her first marathon. She was prudent to have chosen a 10 km run and heeded the advice of some veteran runners, to stay at the '10 km range', at the first attempt.

Shalini was up to get ready quite early in the morning. She was excited to be active in such an event. Though this too was a race, Shalini was only competing with herself, unlike in the past. She was relieved by that competition. All these years, she was seen competing with rival projects for grabbing resources, budgets, and highlight spaces. The run which she was about to undergo did not wear those contours. She was happy and raring to run.

To enable her run well, Shalini had adopted a balanced training.

Balance exercises can help you keep your balance at any age. Older adults, especially, may think about regularly doing exercises to keep or improve balance. This is important because balance tends to worsen with age. But anyone can be helped by balance training. It can help steady the core muscles.

Shalini had understood the essence of this, and with this balanced training and regular jogging, she readied herself for her first run.

She freshened up, dressed herself in a black suit and pressed the pedal to reach the race venue. Santosh joined her to cheer her. When they reached the venue, they saw a human sea, energised on an early Sunday morning. It was an electrifying atmosphere. The clarion call time for the race was a few minutes away, and young enthusiasts were making the budding runners warm up before they could start sprinting. The crowd had a mix of participants, those expert marathon runners who would run a full marathon, some who were regulars but limited themselves to half the distance and some like Shalini, beginners who wanted to stretch their limits.

Shalini got hold of her practice group, and they clustered together and waited for the bugle whistle. As it flagged, Shalini gathered a steady pace, almost a repetitive, gentle, cyclical leg work, which gradually started to cut off the lap distance. She was around her running mates, though a few of them, who were regular attendees, surged ahead.

As the race progressed, Shalini began to realise the efforts required to keep her going. She started to feel cramped. She was bewildered to experience that difficulty during this actual performance, whereas she fared much better during the drills. She began to feel exhausted and weak after around the 6 km mark. She was on the return route but felt like quitting.

She was running with her head down, trying to purchase strength, will and gumption to keep running. As she was mumbling forward, she thought that even this area chosen had begun to fail her. She was on the cusp of being rendered a failure even there. She was once again perturbed by the test of life. Going away from the stage of challenges, she wanted to be emancipated from their clutches, but there on the street, trying to run hard, pump oxygen into lungs and lunge forward, she was feeling trapped. 'Life can't exist without tests and challenges,' she thought to herself.

She was pondering deep inside, but unknowingly cutting off the distance to reach the finishing line, even without her knowledge. She was picking fresh bottles at water stations, gulping some and pouring the rest on her to keep her cool. She now felt like she had cramps in her calves, and her shin bones began to ache. However, she somehow bought mental strength and grit to keep going. As she kept stretching, Shalini entered the last lap on the ground.

As she was on the ground for the last lap, and found many athletes running and scurrying to breast the finishing tape, a sudden gust of energy flew through her, she as if bit her teeth in determination and propelled herself to lunge forward. Almost on the verge of collapsing, Shalini crossed the finishing line. As she was thirty to forty meters away from the finish, she heard her buddies cheering her, clapping for her to reach their side. That made Shalini put her last gush. It was only a ten-kilometre run, which hundreds of runners had also completed that day along with her, but it was special for her.

It was special since it was an area which she had sculpted for herself after leaving her earned career.

It was special for her because she wanted to prove she could achieve, to her and to the world.

It was special because she wanted to believe that she could do something else, noteworthy, apart from her software career.

It was special because it was achieved by overcoming all the mental challenges thrown at her.

It was special for her.

Santosh was very happy for her.

Shaunak

Shaunak could not express the right emotions when Yeshwant passed away. He had mixed feelings. He was flown to Mumbai for the last sight of his grandfather. He stumbled over the condolence formalities, had some cosy moments with his cousin, tried to be nice to his grandmother, and flew back to Bengaluru to take up his further course.

Shaunak's relation with Sayona had begun to flourish. Now, even Sayona would get his occasional calls after they left college. He did not go intimate with her on the phone, but wanted the conversation to continue, even without any meaningful agenda. That might be called the beginning of love, he sometimes felt.

Shaunak was now on the verge of completing his graduation, and he, with his homemaker mother, started to scout for his further education abroad. Though he was initially uneasy by Shalini leaving her job and staying home, he was now getting used to her presence, and had started to get more confident in her. Santosh, despite that long stay with Shaunak when Shalini was in Mumbai, did not have the easiest access to his son. That too made Shaunak get even closer to his mother.

Shaunak wanted to express his feelings. He was confused if he should share with Tushar or Shalini. Ever since Shalini started to stay home, he began to feel more comfortable interacting with her. So, he decided to share his feelings about Sayona with her. If he were to do that, it would have been the biggest gain for Shalini in earning enough confidence and trust with her son, to be worthy of being shared his intimate feelings with her, due to her close availability.

On one such evening, when the sun was setting behind their house, and twilight was spread over their balcony, Shalini and Shaunak were sitting and trying to figure out avenues for him to push abroad, overlooking that twilight. They had narrowed on the Netherlands as a country, and some courses offered in it, as the least resistance path, given his academic record and eligibility. They together tapered down to four or five cities in the Netherlands, including Rotterdam, Hague, and Amsterdam. Shalini was eager to get him abroad and carefully weighed his chances with those universities, for his background. She started to feel better as she juxtaposed them both, the performance and requirements, and found an acceptable overlay. Shalini had however, given up the USA dream.

Shaunak copied all details into his laptop notes for further action for a possible fall admission. His overall body language was bubblier, spirited, and ecstatic over the last few days. Shalini had not missed it either. She was trying to extrapolate and was trying to imagine Shaunak bitten by the syndrome suitable to his age, but with less conviction, and only broad surmises.

Until Shaunak opened to her. He had rehearsed about how he would disclose and relay his condition to Shalini over the previous few days.

"Mamma, I wanted to share something with you. I do not know if I should be talking to you on this, but I want to admit that I have started to like Sayona. Her presence takes me to a different, nice world," Shaunak revealed.

Shalini was pleasantly spellbound. She was imagining something happening to her son, and could faintly make out with his demeanour, the last few days. But she had no conviction beyond this guess and had not foreseen it could be Sayona. She was closely following him to check if she could extract some meat, but that day, Shaunak himself unlocked the vault and accommodated Shalini in his effervescent state.

She had mixed feelings about comprehending this new side of Shaunak. One rests in solace if the thought is only an inkling. However the curiosity to ascertain the suspicion or the reason for anxiety is high, and often exciting, and once that conjecture is ascertained and truth is revealed, newer thought-challenges take charge.

Shalini was curiously anxious about Shaunak's developments, changes in his behaviour and was enjoying that anxiety, tongue in cheek. But once Shaunak bared her all, she got worked up and began to think loudly. She was aware that such premises do occur and could be ephemeral, but she just wondered if that had earned serious proportions, as those might have brought some resistance to Shaunak's going abroad to study more. She gathered her wits to stay afloat.

She said," My boy! What an assertion this sounds! Shaunu, I always thought you would walk that lane, but at the same time, I also felt you would not. I have known her for the last two-three years, and she has come across as a good girl. She has come to our home a few times, but I could not read too much into her visits. Are you feeling too intense for her?

"Mamma, I do not know how I can express this, but she makes me feel good. I like to be around her, and I think she likes it too."

"Well, young man, you seem to have fallen in love," the mother jibed back. "You are grown-up, mature and an adult too, but give this a good thought before you can really say, this is it."

"Sayona is a good girl, and I have seen her many times. She comes across a well-cultured and soft-spoken girl, but first, both of you talk over and see if you both are in unison. If you need more, feel free to empty more. I leave it to you for the time being. "

Shaunak was relieved to have confessed this to Shalini. In fact, as he disclosed and asserted this to Shalini, it was a confession and admission to himself. He wanted to express this so that he would admit to himself, too. He started to feel more for Sayona.

Shalini left the place for some other chores and to hand over Shaunak some private space. Shaunak too, perhaps wanted it. He took his phone and dialled Sayona. For the first time, he had a new spring in his voice when he spoke to her.

Sayona was pleased to hear his voice, and she rode through the flowery lanes of love. She started to get affirmation that Shaunak had started to reciprocate her feelings. Neither of them had expressed to the other their love for each other.

Shaunak started to float in the sixth heaven after the phone call. He wanted to meet Sayona as early as she could, see her, feel her, smell her, and possibly touch her.

The next day, he got up and finished his daily chores more lavishly than usual and reached the dining table.

As he caught Shalini's eye, he almost blushed. He was surprised by his own reaction. He was bold enough to proclaim it to his mother the other day, and there he was succumbing to the emotion the next day. He laughed to himself.

Shaunak and Sayona kept getting closer and mutually aligned. He started to get too entangled with her. One day, Shalini sat down to review his progress on his master's education and their plans of Netherlands, Saunak got troubled.

He was merrily traversing a serene path of evolving love, and his mother brought him down to the thorned, barbed lane of hardship and labour.

Why Shalini still wanted him to go overseas for higher education was the inherent question in his mind, but he knew that Shalini had wanted that to happen for the last several years. Sayona's was just a recent phenomenon.

He had seen Sayona's entry as a stroke of fortune to get his mother's focus blurred, and with the help of which he could lead a different path which could have been traversed with lesser throughput, efforts, and onus.

He found himself trapped between two paths and felt each path was exclusive and independent of the other. He got sandwiched between a supposedly merrier and a less strenuous path involving Sayona in his life and absenting himself from the current stage for a spell abroad, at least for some period.

Both scenarios could have co-existed, but Shaunak had gotten into a groove to embrace and evaluate each exclusive of the other. His frame of mind initially made him feel he had to choose one at the expense of the other. He was also aware that if he chose to go abroad for further studies, he would have needed to prove himself all over again, this time with even higher intensity. He tried in his mind to use Sayona's shield to save him for proving his performance, anew. It was an overtly simple but strangely a complicated matter for him.

It was even perhaps the symptom of indecision. Shaunak's inability to choose, prioritize and act, meandered around him to bring up excuses and reasons. There was no reason to be confused, perturbed or stressed out. But he did. He knew he could not decide. He did not want to decide. He thought if he extended his leaning to Sayona, Shalini would eventually decide against his going abroad, and that would have suited him.

He felt that he wanted to extend his association with Sayona and was delirious with that thought on one side. But the future obligations in both cases started to make him jittery. That had also started to make him even more circumspect about going further with his relationship with Sayona. He knew that if he decided, he would have needed to stand by the decision and deliver on the expectations of the decision.

He finally reconciled with himself and opted for Shalini to decide for him and take that onus upon herself. He was freaked out by this thought and reached out to his mother for help.

Santosh

At his age, many men undergo a crisis. They are self-sufficient, have already achieved a few things in life, are successful, but still miss something. They try to search for solace, but struggle to reach. They start to get impatient, restless, itchy, and even get into cheerless moods. It is a passing phase. It was during that phase that Santosh had bumped into Yogeshwar.

He was content now that Shalini was getting in her groove, Yashoda possessed no immediate signs of worry, and Shaunak was about to complete his graduation and begin his new life phase. He was feeling lighter by relaxing with these consolations. The curtain raiser by Yogeshwar and his further reading and assimilation of the deep insights of life made him feel less complicated, and his tendency to expect more from life slowly began to moderate.

But nothing stays permanently good. Things change. They change quickly.

Yashoda's condition worsened, and she was suspected of having a progressive stage of Alzheimer's and exhibited hallucinations. Madhusudan first tried to manage and perhaps hid them from Santosh, but they spiralled so fast that it became more evident in her behaviour. He tried to manage at his level, but was ineffective and hassled out.

Madhu finally resigned, accepted the condition, and informed Santosh. He called Santosh on one of the Saturdays. Madhu said," Santosh, are you free for a while?"

Santosh found his tone very alarming. He said, "Baba, I am free. What is the matter? Is all ok? How is Aai?"

Madhu hesitantly replied," Beta, Aai is not ok. She has been experiencing hallucinations and has become forgetful over the last few months. I thought initially that it was old age, but her hallucinations have only increased. She talks with imaginary people who are found sitting on the ceiling fans or empty sofas. She gets verbally aggressive with them and abuses them. Sometimes, she darts to harm them. I am feeling very concerned for her. I tried to manage, but I cannot manage her independently now. Can you come here? She needs to visit a doctor."

Santosh said, "I was fearing this during each visit in the last few months. I had feared for the worse and the worst is happening soon. Baba, do not worry, I will come there, and we shall consult a doctor who can help us diagnose her and help with some treatment as required. Till then, take care, both of you. Is Aai around? Can I speak with her?"

"She is asleep. She was too tired." Madhu resigned.

As he hung up, Santosh went deep into his pensive self and shared these new developments with Shalini. He had to go to Mumbai as soon as he could, but getting leave after so many leaves in the past few months was not going to be easy. He thought he would work from Mumbai for a few days, but he feared that the doctor visits, tests, and other treatments could eat him up. He would need a hiatus from work to get to the core of the new problem.

Shalini offered him to volunteer herself and travel to Mumbai and take care of all the necessities. Santosh, for a moment, felt obliged and relaxed, but soon he realised that it was she who single-handedly fought on all fronts when it was her father, so it should have been he who should be handling the problem when it arose for his mother. He should have accepted Shalini's offer, as after all, Yashoda was also her mother-in-law, and Shalini was free.

Strange complications gathered in his mind, and instead of taking Shalini's help that time, he took upon himself more burden and challenge to break a few shackles, which was perhaps unnecessary.

Santosh flew to Mumbai, got Yashoda checked by a psychiatrist and got her Dementia confirmed.

The diagnosis of Dementia involved a comprehensive evaluation process that included a medical history review, physical examinations, psychiatric evaluations, and cognitive and imaging tests. Santosh was expecting better results at each appearance of these tests, but the tests were honest in confirming her symptoms.

Dementia is the result of changes in certain brain areas that cause neurons and their connections to stop working properly. Why these changes happen in some people but not others is a subject of research, but Yashoda was one of them where changes were happening quite fast.

His contentment, his moderation and the recently acquired implicit and spiritual understanding of life got severely tested.

When matters were favourable, he exhibited the essence of his newly gained aspects of life with alacrity. But as they began to turn adverse, his real test had begun. His newly established spiritual landscape was shattered in no time. He regained his old mishmash and ambled in a welter of internal conflicts.

He had never really gotten the short end of the stick, but he developed a quick tendency towards self-pity.

Looking at Yashoda's condition, Santosh felt that she could not be left alone with Madhu anymore. He wondered how he could handle that. He thought of taking them both to Bengaluru. Their Bengaluru house was not too big, but neither small and surely not too small to accommodate the ailing parents easily.

Hitherto, he also thought of talking to Shalini. He decided to call her in the night and apprise her of all the developments and his latest thought.

As he was busy thinking, he finished dinner and helped Yashoda and Madhu to clear the leftovers. He also realized that Devayani was away from Mumbai but would soon come back and someday would also require physical assistance there. He got further worked up. It would not have been possible to get all three elderly parents to Bengaluru, even in batches.

Santosh thought of shifting back to Mumbai with Shalini and Shaunak. He also thought of vying to seek a possible transfer to Mumbai or working on a hybrid model, shuttling between Mumbai and Bengaluru. Being at such a senior position in his company would not have impeded this request, but looking at Shalini's case, he was not fully confident it would have worked out seamlessly.

Santosh called Shalini, apprised her of the turn of events and left her with more questions in mind, which he too carried, without sharing his topsy-turvy thoughts that were going on in his mind.

"Let us see how we manage this. Good night, I will leave tomorrow by the morning flight, goodnight" Santosh ended his call on this note.

Santosh was crammed between serpentine thoughts that took possession of his mind, with the recent developments and decline of his mother's health.

AFTERWORD

The Sandwich

The only real luxury is time. You wish you ever had more...

Santosh and Shalini represent the *Sandwich Generation*, the generation X, which is responsible towards their parents and the kids alike. This generation is aged in its 50s and faces the challenge to shape the lives of their children and confront the deteriorating health of their parents.

This generation is reared with a very robust value system inherited from their earlier generations, and this keeps them honest in fulfilling their responsibilities towards either of their dependent generations. They have spent most of their adolescence with the kin and hence are competent to think beyond themselves.

They are keen too to extract their flourishing careers and are on the verge of reaching their pinnacle at work. Their children are about to make strides in life, and they feel it dutiful to guide them well to introduce them to *Life*. Their parents are rapidly ageing and even start to exhibit child-like obstinacies. They are needed to walk a tight rope, with a brain-scratching balancing act.

Santosh and Shalini are perfect epitomes of this sandwich generation. They are mindful of their responsibilities but also get swayed by the compulsions of the daily grind, interwoven with personal ambitions and milestones.

Both Shalini and Santosh were keyed to the progress of their son, wanted Shaunak to thrive, get noticed by his academic progress and embrace opportunities that came his way, gamely.

Even without their knowing, they would juxtapose the fledgling career of Shaunak with someone like Tushar, and get worked up by the relative comparisons that should have never existed. That, along with their compulsions at the job, kept them concerned, uneasy and distressed. The predominance of these pseudo-concerns would keep them hunting for bigger moments of joy and often rob them small happy events, which should have been embraced and cherished during the otherwise tumultuous journey. *Pity!!*

Each of them had their turn to attend their sick old parents. As society evolved over the last four to five decades, like most others at their age, they were staying away from their parents.

At the beginning of this dissociation, and during the early part of the two-three-decade period when they had moved to stay away, their parents were initially still relatively younger. This younger couple then had focused solely, on achieving their careers, building their personalities, amassing wealth and had readied to present their son to the world.

As Shaunak grew, albeit with a lot of questions around, Madhu, Yashoda and Devayani started to slide down in health, rapidly. In fact, Yashwant had gotten consumed by old age. Without expressing overtly, Santosh and Shalini both had realised that the parents were on a steady path of waning, till the worst would happen soon, again, but eventually.

However, they never shrugged their responsibilities off, and wanted to stretch long, put their best feet forward to aid the older clan in their last days.

Likewise, there are many couples of their age who have settled, but overseas. Their overseas settlement hands them a spooky geographical defence. They can hide behind it to excuse themselves from the onus of managing the old age responsibilities, *en persona*.

All gung-ho! This section of emigrants once took reciprocative care of their parents, also made regular annual visits, and the parents, too, felt absorbed. But as they grew in age with their parents, their kids grew too and the dimension of time made certain irreversible changes.

The Shalinis and Santoshes have fewer excuses to hide behind and are confronted to take steps that could change their course of lives. However, some emboldened and instated set of comrades defy such challenges, continue their existing way of life and trust in time to take its own course.

Well, that is one way!

Elsewhere, some react to the shifting scenarios and change.

Santosh thought of the change. He wanted to convince Shalini to change, too.

Change!

So that they could handle their future tasks better?

Shalini heard Santosh out.

'Moving to Mumbai!' she shuddered at the idea.

She has just started a new chapter of life, re-establishing herself in the newly incorporated style of life. She had put in some serious efforts and had sculpted her new space. She was asked to dislodge it herself, all so soon.

What a tragedy!!

She at first rebelled. She sided with herself and gave a cold shoulder to Santosh.

"Why now, Santosh? I think I have just found my feet again," She argued.

She knew she was being too self-focused, but she also thought, if it was for a change, she deserved it first.

"I understand you, Shalini. I am feeling terrible to ask you to be removed from your position. I am feeling cruel with this proposal to you. But I thought and thought and thought over it. I cannot find any better option than this, unless we choose to ignore the situation in Mumbai. Our conscience will not easily let us either. It is my Aai today, it could be yours tomorrow, even my father is queued in," Santosh related in a very sombre voice.

Shalini, on hearing this, had a moment of realisation and looked into Santosh's eyes. He had all intent and resignation in his eyes. They were earnest and imploring. Santosh, too, would have needed to break away from his space and garner a new zone for his future. He would have needed macho tasks to manage at both Mumbai and Bengaluru, if that need arose then. He was readying for that as he thought of this change.

Shalini pitied Santosh. She began to decipher the logic and thought behind Santosh's proposal. Santosh always displayed an uncanny knack for scheming things which could never be contested on logic and rationality, even though that was unpopular. His ordeals in his office and his career often exhibited this flavour.

Shalini, on the other hand, with a lot of efforts it was that she, had put herself back on track, a new track, and it was being asked to be rerouted.

She wanted to be nice, but also nice to herself.

She wanted to ready herself to sacrifice, but struggled.

"I understand, Santosh, where you are coming from," She acknowledged. Silence followed this, a longer one.

After a lull, as both were short of immediate responses and decisions, they both agreed not to conclude anything then. They both thought they deserved more time, despite not having much.

Santosh got up, took sluggish steps to his bar, and reached out for the bottle which came to his hand first, poured into the glass without bothering to measure, and immersed himself in the mystic flavours. When the brain finds roadblocks, the mind dunks into the mysterious.

Good for Santosh?

But Shalini?

She did not earn any such luxuries. She had to delve into the matter, in a sober state and think a way out. Thinking a way out meant agreeing with Santosh.

The play of the gunas was prominently visible. The preponderance of the *Sattva* guna made both feel it necessary to be with their ailing parent(s), to empathise with their sufferings and contribute in their best way to aid them out, especially in their waning phase. The *Rajas* guna had defiantly arisen to overpower the *Sattva*, by contrasting to this, and highlighting the sacrifices, displacements both would have needed to undergo, should they have decided to move out, at the cost of their supposed future achievements. That made them testy, anxious, perturbed, and indecisive.

The intrinsic dominance and the organic chemistry of the gunas are integral to each mortal of the universe. Their interplay sways the character into different thoughts, deeds, and acts; good, bad and the ugly. However, the purer the gunas, the more pristine their impact.

As the *Sattva* and *Rajas* toggled and brawled amongst each other for both Shalini and Santosh, the *Tamas* wrested control and tried to pull over, instilling unpreparedness and moments of uncanny rebellion. The interlock between the gunas kept them both hung in abeyance. Both struggled to make a quick decision. Deciding was essential; deciding quickly was paramount.

Such situations take charge and come out of nowhere, anytime, without a warning. That stirs up the inner formation and forcefully drags one to participate in the tournament of change, unwillingly, as often.

Why would both Santosh and Shalini heed the call for change? The conscience which flourished by the dawn of *Sattva* made them responsive and responsible to respond to the call. But, as often as it happens, the intellect of a man with unstable thoughts, unthinking and wishfulness is disturbed in many ways. The circumstances and the gunas completely sandwich one, and contest and conquer to arrive at a rational solution.

In such cases, it is always advisable to get out of their clutches and influence, and become self-reliant and get oriented to the real self.

Easier said than done!

All then stays important is to take a righteous decision, which demands a sane, moral, and virtuous state of mind, the mind which collaborates with the intellect.

Santosh was by then swimming like a tipsy turtle, and Shalini was staring and digging deep within. They were struggling but self-burdened to break the barriers. They were, at the same time, thinking of themselves, their stage of life, and about Shaunak too. Shalini was also thinking about Sayona. The moment they thought it was beginning to get easier to decide by adopting an uncomplicated approach, the bewilderment that arose due to the sight of all the fringe areas of their thought bandwagon, and their dreams for their son, all made it obscure, congested and challenging for them again, to decide.

They also interacted and reminisced amongst themselves about their peers, some of them around, some of them who had settled abroad and those who had to face similar encounters concerning their inner families. Quietly inside, they attempted to read their lives and tried to search for a method. *Good try!* but such methods are not universal. Even the curious case of the childless couple, Yogini and Govind, quickly scrolled over Shalini's mind. Though studying others' lives might be easy, matching theirs is not.

Some deeper thinking took them closer to the decision, and again took them far, and they kept swaying, thinking, and weighing what they thought. Like a few constants of nature, choice is a constant. It always exists.

Not deciding was also a choice,

Only if they had the luxury of time!